"Jonny, I can't believe you remembered that crazy pumpkin top I wore that day, back in high school."

Her gaping mouth drew into a smile. "I think I blocked that gaudy thing from my memory."

But he hadn't. When she'd hoisted the carton of food from the trunk, the sunlight hit her auburn hair and streaked it with gold, the color of leaves at the height of autumn. It had taken his breath away. He'd just turned fourteen, and Neely had become his first secret love.

Neely shook her head as a soft chuckle escaped her. "Why would you remember something like that?"

Talk about reality. The truth smacked him in the head and slipped to his tongue. "Because I had the biggest crush on you."

Her hand flew up. "What are you saying? You had a crush on me?" She searched his eyes before she burst into a laugh. "You were a pesky kid."

To her maybe, but to him, he was a man in love....

Books by Gail Gaymer Martin

Love Inspired

*Loving Treasures
*Loving Hearts
Easter Blessings
"The Butterfly Garden"
The Harvest
"All Good Gifts"
*Loving Ways
*Loving Care
Adam's Promise
*Loving Promises
*Loving Feelings
*Loving Tenderness
†*In His Eyes*
†*With Christmas in His Heart*
†*In His Dreams*
†*Family in His Heart*
Dad in Training
Groom in Training
Bride in Training
**A Dad of His Own
**A Family of Their Own
Christmas Gifts
"Small Town Christmas"
**A Dream of His Own
Her Valentine Hero

Steeple Hill Books

The Christmas Kite
Finding Christmas
That Christmas Feeling
"Christmas Moon"

*Loving
†Michigan Islands
**Dreams Come True

GAIL GAYMER MARTIN

is an award-winning author, writing women's fiction, romance and romance suspense with over three million books in print. Gail is the author of twenty-eight worship resource books and *Writing the Christian Romance* released by Writer's Digest Books. She is a cofounder of American Christian Fiction Writers, a member of the ACFW Great Lakes Chapter, member of RWA and three RWA chapters.

A former counselor and educator, Gail has enjoyed this career since her first book in 1998. This book is her fiftieth novel. When not writing, she enjoys traveling, speaking at churches and libraries and presenting writing workshops across the country. Music is another love, and she spends many hours involved in singing as a soloist, praise leader and choir member at her church, where she also plays handbells and hand chimes. She sings with one of the finest Christian chorales in Michigan, the Detroit Lutheran Singers. A lifelong resident of Michigan, she lives with her husband, Bob, in the Detroit suburbs. Visit her website at www.gailmartin.com, write to her at P.O. Box 760063, Lathrup Village, MI 48076, or at authorgailmartin@aol.com.

Her Valentine Hero

Gail Gaymer Martin

Love Inspired

ISBN-13: 978-0-373-87795-9

HER VALENTINE HERO

This edition published by arrangement with Love Inspired Books.

www.LoveInspiredBooks.com

Printed in U.S.A.

"I know the plans I have for you," declares the Lord,
"plans to prosper you and not to harm you,
plans to give you hope and a future."
—*Jeremiah* 29:11

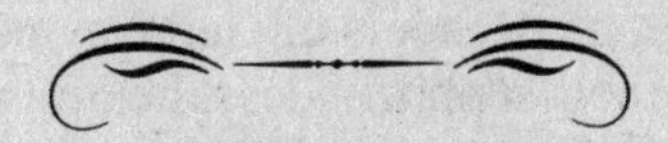

Thanks to writer friend and E.R. doctor Mel Hodde, who provided me with medical information and validated information I'd already collected. Thanks to Gary Lowry, who read my sports scenes and gave me an A-okay. Again, thanks to my Facebook group, Readers of Gail Gaymer Martin's Books, for their support, ideas, helpful comments and wonderful reviews. If authors didn't have readers, what good would a book be? Thanks to my agent, Pam Hopkins, and as always, my deepest thanks and love to my husband, Bob. Without his support and patience (especially that), I wouldn't be the writer I am today.

Chapter One

Neely Andrews forced her legs to keep moving. One more lap and she'd take a break. Her tendency to add pounds to her five foot six frame provided perfect motivation to exercise. But since she'd been back in Ferndale for nearly seven weeks, she hadn't exercised at all except for running up and down her father's staircase. In Indianapolis, she'd joined a gym. Now she was worried about her dad's recovery from a serious heart attack. Fitness had gone out the window, and weight had flown in. Running the high school track wasn't the answer to her total workout needs, but it was better than nothing.

Although staying in Indianapolis might have been wiser, since she had the lead on another job, she couldn't ignore her need to be closer to her father and widowed sister. Each time she thought about Ashley's loss, Neely's layoff became as unimportant as a lost penny, and though home brought back some darker thoughts, she focused on the brighter memories of friendships and happy times that still made her smile.

Fighting the desire to give her body a rest, Neely steeled herself and pushed forward, her lungs burning. Short of her goal, she nearly tripped over a shoelace splayed at her feet. She came to a stop, propped her hands on her thighs and braced her winded body to catch her breath. When she grasped the lace to retie her shoe, perspiration rolled down her forehead and stung her eyes. She lifted the bottom of her T-shirt and brushed the dampness away.

A wolf whistle jerked her upward, and she dropped the hem of her shirt. Across the field, boys were spilling from the school, wearing shoulder pads and carrying helmets. Two faced her, gawking. She let out a groan. Football practice. Another wolf whistle spurred her to turn away and ignore the silliness. She lowered her eyes to her plump legs, bare beneath a pair of running shorts. Who knew football practice began in August?

Her mind drifted back to the years she'd spent at this high school, but time fogged her mind. Memories of special occasions—some good, some bad—had glided or stumbled through her thoughts once in a while, but football practice hadn't made an impact. Didn't matter anyway. After fifteen years, school procedures had probably changed. Everything had changed.

A shrill whistle caught her attention. She looked toward the team and saw a man strutting onto the field. He glanced her way, said something to the boys, and before she could move, he headed in her direction. She focused on her lace. No doubt she would get a lecture from the coach for being on his turf. While she hurried to retie her shoe, his voice reached her. "Ma'am."

What happened to Ms.? She tilted her head sideways noticing his long stride toward her. His build looked trimmer than a football player's, but beneath his T-shirt she recognized a solid swell of muscles. His frame would look appropriate on a basketball court.

"Ma'am, would you mind leaving the field?"

What happened to please?

"You're distracting the boys."

She what? She straightened, embarrassed at his comment but, more so, irritated. "Sorry, I would have run the track this morning when I drove here earlier, but then I had to fight off the band. Apparently that's when they practice." When he drew close enough for to her to see his face, her heart tripped.

His squint grew to a wide-eyed stare. "Whoa! This can't be Steely Neely?"

She couldn't believe this good-looking specimen was her friend Rainie's pesky kid brother. The only person she knew who would call her the concocted name was Jonny Turner. In the past, she would have shot out her typical insult, but "If it isn't the conehead" faded from her mind. When she looked into his handsome face, she had all she could do to keep her mouth from gaping as widely as his.

"Jonny Turner. You're kidding me." She gazed upward at the six-foot-plus hunk of man with the blue eyes she could never forget. Blue like a crystal lake. It had been Jonny's saving attribute, and she'd told him so years earlier.

"How about Jonathan or Jon." He grinned, obviously enjoying her startled expression. "Jonny's long gone."

"Jon not Jonny? I don't know." She gave him a dubious look. "But here's a deal—only if you drop the ridiculous Steely Neely. It's stupid."

"No, it's accurate." He sent her a crooked smile. "Even when we were kids, I'd never known a person as determined as you are. You were as strong-willed as steel."

She rolled her eyes, hoping he got the point, but showing her usual disdain with him was losing the battle.

His grin remained as if he hadn't noticed her eye-rolls. "Sis told me you were back in town. And I hear you're her maid of honor."

Neely managed an agreeable nod, though she was still

in a tailspin. Maid of honor seemed a sad title for a thirty-two-year-old woman. Most of her high school friends would expect her to be dubbed the matron of honor by now. But finding Mr. Right hadn't happened, not since her days with Erik Cross. She cringed. He'd been Mr. Wrong.

Jonny's eyes brightened. "And if I'm right, maid of honor means you're still—"

"Right again." She rolled her eyes for a second time, not happy with the gleam in his. He'd always rebutted her verbal jabs with "you'll never find a man with that attitude." He'd been way too accurate.

"What are you doing here?" She waved her hand toward the gawking teens watching them.

"I was going to ask you the same question." He motioned to the strip of track. "I teach phys ed and coach football and basketball." This time he rolled his eyes. "That's obvious, isn't it? But you again, that's a different story. Why are you running on my track?"

"It's a long story." And not a story she wanted to tell him. The more she looked at him the more tongue-tied she became. "Rainie didn't mention you were teaching now." Or that you'd turned into a great-looking man.

"Why would Lorraine talk to you about me?" He chuckled. "Or have you forgotten your lovable animosity?" He shifted to face his gawking team, and blew his whistle.

She pressed her hands over her ears, blocking the shrill assault on her eardrums.

He cupped his hands around his mouth like a megaphone. "Push-ups. Twenty." He held up both hands, fingers spread and acted out his order. Their groans sounded across the distance.

She lowered her hands. "Can you warn me when you're going to blow that thing?"

"Sorry." He dropped the whistle, and it bounced against

his chest before hanging in place. His eyes shifted from the team to her. "I need to get back to my boys, but…" He touched her arm. "I wanted to say I'm sorry about your dad. I heard it was a bad one."

His sincere turn-about caught her off-guard. "It was. Really bad. He lost a lot of his heart function. Now that Mom's gone I need to keep him healthy." Watching her dad trudging up and down the stairs for something he'd forgotten wasn't part of her health plan for him. On the other hand, convincing him to use the guest room on the first floor was. Yet so far her attempt had failed. Maybe that's where she'd inherited her determination. He stood as firm as a rock. She sighed. "Running the stairs for him is the only exercise I've gotten since I came home. That's why I'm jogging around the track."

He wrapped his arm around her and gave her shoulder a hug. "Exercise is good." He squeezed her again before dropping his arm. "We have a new gym in town, Tone and Trim Fitness Center. I go there. You might want to give it a try."

"Are you telling me I can't run your track?" She arched a brow, a little irked at his suggestion.

He grinned. "You can run anytime you want except when my boys are on the field. You're a real distraction."

His expression caused heat to rise up her neck. "I'll take your suggestion into advisement." But a fitness center cost money, and right now she was jobless.

He gave her a wink. "I need to get back to my team. I wish we had more time to talk." His eyes captured hers, and a tender expression washed over his face. "I can't believe it's you." He took off running backward, his eyes still on her, but when he spun around, he came to a halt.

Neely winced, thinking he might trip with the abrupt stop, but he didn't, he turned back to her again.

"I'll be done here in an hour or so. How about coffee or even dinner. Will you join me?"

Ten years ago the idea would have been ludicrous, but at the moment, looking at those eyes had roused her interest even though she still couldn't accept he was the new improved Jonny. A crazy memory popped into her mind, and she jabbed her fist into her hip. "You poured sand in my hair when I was twelve."

His jaw dropped before a glint sprang to his eyes. "Accident, or maybe I wanted you to appreciate my new dump truck." He gave her a wink. "Whichever, I promise I'll never do it again."

The wink sent prickles down her arm, and a witty retaliation failed her.

He started his backward walk toward his team. "So what about joining me?"

His easy spirit and charm made her head spin while curiosity got the better of her. "Sounds nice, Jonny. I'm staying at my dad's. You remember where it is?"

"How could I forget?" His backward jog picked up. "Give me a couple hours. Let's call it dinner."

He darted off, and she watched him go, still trying to turn that good-looking man into Rainie's brother who'd been the bane of her teen years. And if that didn't confuse her, her heartbeat, flitting like a bird in spring, did.

Jon strode along the sidewalk beside Neely, amazed that she'd agreed to have dinner with him. When they were growing up, she avoided him every chance she had. But he couldn't blame her. He was four years younger than she, and obnoxious. Boys who'd just learned about girls and had to deal with the first twitches of testosterone failed to make wise decisions when it came to falling in love. Neely had hung in his mind forever. And today, Neely, the woman, tightened the noose without knowing. He'd thought about her all these years, never suspecting the Lord would bring her back into his life. But here she was.

In his peripheral vision, he drank in her profile, the tilt of her well-shaped nose, the fullness of her lips, the rounded shape of her cheek molding into her defined jaw. His hopes lifted knowing he would see her around town—maybe even back on the track—but he wanted so much more, and most important, he needed to test the waters. "Are you looking forward to seeing Erik at Rainie and Ty's engagement party?"

Her eyes darkened. "Erik? You mean Erik Cross? Don't tell me he's still in town." A look of panic filled her face.

Though her expression heightened his confidence, it confused him. "Erik joined his dad's company after college so he's still in the area." He studied her, trying to make sense out of what had just happened. Panic didn't seem appropriate. "Sorry I mentioned him. I didn't realize you had bad—"

Her distraught look remained. "Maybe you didn't know—you were so young—but I broke off our relationship." She shrugged. "He started talking marriage, and I realized I had a whole life in front of me."

He'd known about her breakup with Erik. Rainie and she had talked about it, and he'd overheard some of their conversations, but Neely had been the one to end it so why did it still hold a sting? Her attitude turned him upside down. It didn't quite make sense. To him real love meant he would have a whole world in front of him to be with the woman he loved. "You two were a thing back in high school."

"I know. We broke up just before he left for college."

Her comment seemed an afterthought, yet he struggled with her strained expression. "Sorry, Neely. I knew you weren't together because I knew you hadn't married him. But I didn't know you had bad feelings."

She shook her head. "I need to get over it." She averted her eyes and kicked at a stone on the sidewalk. "Where is this restaurant, anyway?"

"Right up ahead." He pointed to the purple-and-green-striped awning a block away. "It's called Pronto." He slipped his hand to her shoulder, wanting to ease her edginess. "Can we forget my earlier reference and cheer up?"

She tilted her head toward him. "I am cheery, but I'm not happy to hear Erik's coming to the party. Why was he invited?"

"He's a friend of Ty's."

She drew up her shoulders. "I'll just steer clear of him. I'm not in the mood for auld lang syne." Her lips curved to a faint grin. "You know what I mean?"

He agreed, but he really didn't know what she meant unless her reference hinted at Erik's problem. Cheating on his wife had ended Erik's marriage. Maybe it ended Neely's relationship with him, too.

They walked the rest of the way in silence, and he was grateful when they'd reached the restaurant. He opened the door, wishing he could start their visit again. "How about over there?" He motioned to the empty table.

She nodded and followed his direction without comment, and once seated, she studied the menu while he studied her. Being with Neely seemed like a dream. Years ago he'd been Rainie's brother. Today he'd become an equal. At least an equal in his mind. "Does having dinner with me seem strange?" He lowered his menu to the table.

Her head jerked upward as color tinted her face. "You must have read my mind."

He wished he could. "No, but I'm a good guesser."

A grin flickered on her lips. "I'm trying to acclimate

myself to the situation. If it weren't for your gorgeous eyes, I'd think you were an imposter."

Her resolute gaze nearly caused his undoing. "I hope that's a compliment."

"It is." She turned her attention to the menu.

Aware that he'd reaped a compliment from Steely Neely sent his pulse racing. But then reality brought it to a halt. A compliment was only that. He wanted so much more. "Rainie said you're home to stay."

She inched her head upward as if in thought. "Not sure about the 'to stay' part, but right now I'm home without other plans. I was laid off from Zigman's, and with the economy so bad, I read the writing on the wall. The layoff would be permanent."

"You didn't read the writing well enough, I'm afraid." He hated being the bearer of bad news, but she needed to know.

She tilted her head as if puzzled.

"Michigan's economy is rotten, too."

"I know. It's the pits." Her face shadowed. "It doesn't matter, I guess. I really came back for Dad and my sister. It's been tough for Ashley."

Those feelings were ones he understood. "Losing a husband with a newborn baby is something I can't even wrap my mind around." Neely's expression deepened his sadness.

"Jonny." She gave his arm a pat. "Thanks for caring."

Her hand didn't move, and the warmth radiated to his chest. He looked into her eyes, wishing he could resolve her problems for her.

Something seemed to distract her, and she sat a moment in silence. Finally her face brightened. "Enough about me. Tell me about you."

"What do you want to know?"

"I don't remember your being involved in sports. What made you go into coaching?"

He picked up on her evasion. Talking about him got her off the hook. "Remember what you said. You were older than I was so you probably wouldn't have known what I enjoyed." He twisted the knife a bit. He could play the age game, too.

"I'm not that old." She arched a brow.

He arched his back. "And I'm not that young."

Her face broke into a full smile. "You got me." She rested her cheek on her fist and studied him.

"And I remember a lot of things about you…even at my very young age." He gave the knife another playful thrust.

She didn't flinch. "Go on. You've captured my interest. What do you remember?" She leaned closer and grasped his hand. "This is fun, Jonny."

Fun for her, but serious for him. He wasn't that boy any longer, not by a long shot. He was a man—a football coach with respect from his team and the community—not an irritating kid. And he wanted her to know it. "How about calling me Jon?"

She drew back, releasing his hand. "Jon? That sounds weird." She shook her head. "I'll work on it. That's all I can promise."

Wishing he hadn't jumped at her, he managed a smile. "That's good enough." He grasped the menu, and raked his eyes over the choices, needing time to get his thoughts together.

The tension faded from her face. "No matter what I call you, you'll always be Jonny to me." She rested her hand on his again. "And no more digs."

Relief. He nodded, but his attention had shot to the touch of her hand. Heat from her fingers swam up his arm and into his chest. "Sounds good to me."

Her gaze drifted to the tabletop a moment as a fresh frown sneaked to her lips.

"Neely?"

Her head jerked up, and it took a minute for her eyes to clear. "One more question, and I even hate to ask it."

His pulse skipped as he waited.

She looked away. "This is about Erik."

He figured.

"I'd feel better knowing he's married. He is, isn't he?"

Jon's chest constricted, but the truth needed to be heard. "He was married but not anymore. Erik's divorced."

Her frown deepened. "Divorced?"

He nodded, and slipped his hand from beneath hers to grasp the menu. "We'd better order. I have some errands to run tonight." He could have told her the truth about Erik, but he avoided anything that reeked of gossip, and he saw in her eyes she wanted details.

Neely glanced at her watch before she perused the menu, though her questioning gaze flashed toward him more than once.

He didn't bite. "I'm ready to order. Are you? They have a great Mediterranean platter—grilled chicken, peppers, hummus, orzo or how about Chicken Quesadillas?"

She lowered her eyes to the menu, then closed it, but he could see food wasn't on her mind. Erik was, and she longed to dig deeper. If she learned any more, it wouldn't be from him. He had no interest in discussing Erik's dirty laundry. None at all. His attention remained on her—the girl he'd always sensed was his soul mate.

Chapter Two

Neely stood in the bridal salon dressing room, her gaze on the icy-green silk chiffon fabric shirred at the bodice and falling in soft draping to her feet. She craned over her shoulder to look in the mirror at the back of the gown. In the past week, she'd lost a couple pounds, but that didn't make a dent in where she wanted to be. Running the track at the school had become a problem between the football team and the band. By the time football season was over, she'd have to run in snow.

She gave another glance at the gown from behind, pleased that her additional pounds didn't show from that view. Jonny had mentioned the new fitness center, and if it weren't for the money, she would rush over and sign up, but first she wanted to see what she could manage on her own. So far, she'd pretty much failed.

"Can I come in?" Rainie's voice swept in from behind the curtain.

"Sure." She turned to face the doorway. None of her friends in Indianapolis knew her as well as Rainie. "I love the dress. You made a great choice." She raised her arms at her side, and swished the skirt with a sway. "What do you think?"

Rainie pressed her hand to her heart. “It’s gorgeous, and you look amazing.” She motioned for her to twirl around.

Neely did as she asked, feeling the soft fabric brush against her legs. She hadn’t been in a gown since the senior prom when Erik was at her side. The breakup occurred during the summer before college. She hadn’t planned it. It just happened despite her guilt. The image that clung in her mind was his persistence for getting her in his bed. *Prove your love.* His words still rang in her head. She’d been strong until her senior year when they were preparing for college. He would head for an Ivy League university and she, to a nearby community college for two years. She’d thought giving in would keep him faithful, but she’d been wrong. He’d cheated on her anyway.

Coming home and hearing Erik’s name had dredged up the bad feelings and her guilt. Now she had to work at disposing of them and forgiving herself for her pitiful decision. One thing she’d learned about maturing. Strength and wisdom came with age and experience. At least it had for her, all except one thing. Though she knew the Lord forgave her for her mistake, she hadn’t forgiven herself. But that was years ago, and now she’d learned even more about herself and about men in general. She had her fill of them. Nothing would make her change her—

“Hell-o.”

The singsong greeting jarred her thoughts. She gave Rainie a guilty smile. “I was on a little time travel.”

Rainie tilted her head. “Any place interesting?”

“Not really.” She didn’t want to get into her mental mess even if Rainie was her best friend and her confidant. Her intimate relationship with Erik was the one thing she’d never shared.

“Come on. What were you thinking?”

Her friend’s persistence could drive her loco. “High

school. The prom." She ran her hands along the soft fabric. "That's the last time I wore a formal."

Rainie's grin sank. "You and Erik." She shook her head. "Sorry. I didn't mean to bring that up, but then that should be water over the dam as they say." Her grin returned.

"Lots of water." She managed to grin back. "Jonny told me Erik's divorced."

"Right. He is." Her eyes widened. "When did you see Jon?"

Neely's pulse skipped. "You call him Jon, too."

"What else? Now that he's six foot two and built like an athlete, Jonny doesn't fit him." She curled up her nose. "Don't you think?"

"I suppose, but he'll always be Jonny to me." Her chest tingled, and the reaction jarred her. She pushed the feeling away and gazed down at the gown.

Rainie nodded. "I'm so glad you like the choice. Do you think the bridesmaids will?"

Neely ran her hand down the bodice of the silky fabric. "What's not to like? I think it will flatter most figures."

"I thought so, too."

She turned toward Rainie. "Why didn't you tell me what a great-looking guy Jonny turned out to be?" Another sensation trilled along her skin, like a wisp of hair she tried to brush from her face but could never find.

Her eyes widened. "He's my brother. Why would I tell you about his looks? I don't think about it." She drew back. "Anyway you always called him a pest and ignored him, so why would I mention him?"

Jonny had said the same, and she still didn't have an answer that made sense. Rather than trying to sort it out, she eyed herself in the mirror again. "I can take the gown off, can't I? We both love the style." She turned her back to Rainie, and motioned her to unzip the dress.

When she stepped out of it, Rainie hung it on the hanger and then faced her. "The bridesmaid dresses are just like yours except they'll be a deeper shade of spring green."

"Sounds pretty." Neely stepped into her jeans and pulled them up.

Rainie eyed her a moment. "You still didn't answer my question about Jon. When did you see—"

Neely waved her words away. "On the high school track." As she dressed, she gave her a short summary, anxious to change the topic.

"And you had dinner?" Rainie's eyebrows touched her hairline. "That's interesting."

Her expression roused Neely's curiosity. "Why?"

"I think you're the first girl he's taken to dinner in a long time."

She waited for more, but Rainie just looked at her. "Doesn't he date?"

"A guy that good-looking would, but he never seemed to get serious about any of them until a year or so ago, and then I expected to hear wedding bells."

Her chest constricted, picturing Jonny with a wife.

"He dated Jeannie longer than anyone else."

Neely drew air into her depleted lungs. "Jeannie? Anyone I'd know?"

"I suppose you do. Jeannie Hunt."

"Jeannie Hunt?" The question shot out of her like a bark. "The cutesy little cheerleader from the tenth grade?"

"The same."

That knocked the wind out of her. Now that she thought about it, Jonny hadn't told her anything about himself when they'd talked. She faced the mirror again, eyeing her dark hair, a face that could be lost in a crowd, and a figure that she hid beneath loose fitting apparel like her jogging pants. Jeannie had been a petite blond with curves in the right places and a face that could have been on a Barbie doll. She spun around again. "What happened between them?"

Rainie shrugged. "I don't know. He stopped talking about her, and when I asked, he just blew it off." Rainie slid the curtain aside, and stepped into the alteration room as if the subject had ended.

Neely's mind was stuck with the image of Jonny and the Barbie doll.

Rainie spun around. "Before we leave, would you like a peek at my wedding dress?"

Though her thoughts lingered on other things, she couldn't ignore Rainie's excitement. "I'd love to see it."

Rainie darted away, and as she vanished through the doorway, Neely kept fixating on Jonny. He'd grown into a hunk—a really nice hunk—but what did that have to do with her? No way could she turn her relationship with him into a romance no matter how good-looking or sweet he'd become.

When Rainie returned, Neely slammed the door on her pondering. Seeing her friend's glinting eyes made her focus on the moment. A saleswoman appeared behind her, carrying the wedding dress.

Neely's heart stood still. The soft white gown floated in the woman's arms, organza flanges and tulle swirls of fabric skirt sweeping into a cathedral train. "You'll be the most beautiful bride in the world."

Tears flooded Rainie's eyes, and she wrapped her arm around her friend's shoulders. "One day I'll be your matron of honor, and then it will be your turn to be the most beautiful bride in the world."

The idea warmed her, and she closed her eyes, envisioning her father—healthy and happy—walking her down the aisle. Ahead of her, she gazed at the groom, his eyes tethered to hers, and her heart stopped. She drew in an urgent breath.

"Neely, what's wrong?"

She gathered her wits. "Nothing. I only hope my dad is still alive to see that day."

"Oh, sweetie." Rainie folder her into an embrace, but Neely struggled to clear her mind of the vision she had seen beside the altar. It was Jonny's spectacular blue eyes that drew her down the aisle.

Jon peddled faster, his thoughts keeping up with the bike's speed. Exercise provided therapeutic release to his struggling emotions. He'd always prayed Neely would come back in his life now that age and success were on his side. But he never expected the Lord to answer his far-fetched request.

He gripped the metallic bar, and in a moment eyed his pulse rate. Excellent. He upped the resistance and dug in to the pedals giving the bike another five minutes to deepen the burn. The old motto, no pain no gain, flashed through his thoughts but not nearly as often as Neely's image. Since he'd talked with her, his emotions roller-coastered through his chest until he wanted to rip up the tracks.

With her back in Ferndale his hope rose again. Maybe her return was part of God's plan. Knowing Erik was out of the picture cheered him, too. Now he needed to spend time with her so she could know Jon Turner the man, not Jonny Turner the boy who hung out in the shadows and tripped her up with his attempts to watch her every move. He ran errands for her and Rainie just to spend time with Neely.

In his early twenties, he finally understood what about her mesmerized him. First, she was pretty, like sunshine on dew. He cringed at the poetic thought, but that's what she was like—fresh and open to newness. Even when she put him down, her smile softened the blow, and it felt more playful than serious. And sometimes he had deserved it.

But it wasn't her good looks that interested him. Lots of girls were pretty. Neely showed a depth of spirit that captured him. He admired her determination and her self-reliance. Most of all her generosity. She'd demonstrated the same trait by leaving her life in Indianapolis to come home to her family who needed her.

Slowing the pedals, he let his muscles cool as his mind reverted back to his plan. Somehow he had to get her back into his life. If she bought a gym membership, he could see her here. If not, maybe the church could be their connection. Or maybe a charitable activity. Even as a teenager, Neely involved herself in more charity events than he could count. The idea sent his pulse surging far beyond what registered on the heart rate monitor. He grinned as he slowed, and then stopped. Now to put his plan to work.

While he showered and slipped back into street clothes, he devised his approach. If he wanted to involve Neely in an activity that connected them, he needed a plan, short range and long range.

Plan A would involve fun times. Time to talk. Since exercising seemed one of her goals, he could begin there. When he stepped from the locker room, he eyed the desk, and Cindy flashed him a grin.

He sauntered over, hoping to look casual. "I have a question."

"Anything you want, Jon."

Calling him by his first name tickled him. No one at the center seemed to know who he was, but Cindy always did. "An old friend of mine moved home for a while, and I told her about the fitness center. I wondered if she'd joined."

She tilted her head. "A friend?"

He shrugged. "She's my sister's friend. Neely Andrews. Do you know if she's a member?"

She studied him a minute as if he'd asked for Neely's address or phone number.

"I've known her for years. I'm just curious."

Without a comment, she opened a file on her computer. "She joined three days ago. She hit us on a good day. We were running a special."

"Great." He stepped back, weighing the ogling grin on her face. "Thanks for the information."

"Anything else I can do for you?" She closed the file with a click and rested her cheek on her fist. "Anything. Just ask." She flashed him another smile.

Feeling uneasy, he slipped his hands in his pockets and backed away. "Nothing else today." He spun around and headed out the door, wondering what was up with Cindy.

His uneasiness vanished when he hit the sidewalk. Neely had a membership, and he hoped he'd run into her there, but he feared she'd come during the day when he was at work. Then he'd have to revert to plan B. As yet, he didn't have a solid one. But he'd work on it.

Neely stretched back her shoulders to release the strain. Being away from the gym the past weeks had taken its toll, and though she'd tried running the school track, she didn't have the commitment that investing money motivated. She'd joined the gym a week ago, and already she saw a difference on her scale.

Her legs burning, she forged ahead, determined to focus on the stair machine. She'd jumped from treadmill to bike to weights and now the steps. She hated them, but her personal trainer in Indianapolis explained the importance, for both toning and for general good health. Having someone guide her worked better than wandering from machine to machine with no method.

Although a trainer would be best, it was expensive. She had to be sensible now that her only income was workers' compensation, and she wanted no part in depleting her savings. She longed to buy a house of her own.

The exercise accomplished something else important. It cleared her mind. At home with only her dad to talk with, she'd let herself bog down with thoughts of Erik and her history with him. The memories swelled like an abscess. Instead of the fun memories of their earlier time together, she remembered only the bad ones. After she'd started college, the situation struck her hard. She fought the desire to contact him, but as more time passed, when she finally arrived home, she learned through friends that he'd been dating, and she was frustrated that he'd used her with promises of commitment, and then moved on without making an attempt to win her back.

Since the night she gave in to his pressure, she'd never been the same. Instead of beautiful memories of an intimate relationship between husband and wife, her mind was bogged down with shame and a sense of being soiled. She wondered what Jonny would think if he knew. She could only guess he'd be disappointed since he seemed to think she was so great.

Burying the thoughts for now, she studied her surroundings. Since arriving, her eyes kept shifting to the doorway, and the involuntary reaction irked her. She'd wondered if she would see Jonny one late afternoon, but he hadn't appeared. Disappointment zapped her each time a tall, masculine frame strode through the entrance, and when she focused on the man, she'd see it wasn't Jonny. Then she spent the next few minutes chastising herself for caring who came through the door. Jonny could be a friend. Nothing more.

She eyed her watch and settled on another fifteen minutes, ten to exercise and five to cool down. She tackled the stair machine, keeping her eyes on the digital screen and holding back a groan with each step.

"You've worked up a sweat."

Her heart skipped. Amazed, she lifted her eyes to Jonny's. "I like to call it glowing."

He stood beside the machine, a grin on his face.

"You won't believe this but I was just thinking of—" She caught herself. Jonny would want to know what she was thinking, and when she told him, he would ask, "Why were you thinking of me?" And she didn't know why.

"Thinking of what?"

"Winding down." Saved. She didn't want to lie, but that was also the truth.

"I was doing laps in the pool." He gave a head toss in that direction. "I decided to do something different today." He flexed his shoulders. "Swimming gives different muscles a workout."

She nodded, her concentration failing.

He stood still, watching her as she slowed her steps for the cool down, but her mind slowed, too, and all she could do is gaze at the new Jonny. His gaunt jaw had strengthened and molded into a square chin, today with the hint of dark bristles. She'd never thought of him as rugged, but that's what he'd become—strong features, classically handsome, with well-shaped lips, cheeks with the glint of a dimple, short dark wavy hair contrasting with his amazing blue eyes.

She managed to find her voice. "I took your advice and here I am." She gestured to the workout room. "No personal trainer, but I'm trying to follow the advice from the one I had in Indianapolis."

"They're helpful." He looked thoughtful. "I think you get a free hour of personal training with your membership, don't you?"

"Yes, but I haven't scheduled it yet." She slowed to a stop and stepped off. "I'm finished for today. My muscles can't take another step."

"I know a lot about exercise so if you have any questions, just ask. I keep my boys pretty fit back at school." He dragged the towel from the bar where she'd hung it and daubed her cheeks and forehead before handing it to her.

Her heart skipped, and it irked her. Those unexpected sensations threw her off balance. This was Jonny. She had to remember that. He looked at her as if waiting for a response. "Thanks for the offer and your assistance." She dangled the towel in front of him. "You were very gallant."

"I wouldn't call it 'gallant.' 'Practical' is better. Glow can burn your eyes." He sent her a coy look. "If you're heading for the locker room, I'll walk with you."

She gathered her towel and water bottle, took a long swig, and trudged beside him to the locker room. Her legs trembled with each step, and she wasn't sure if the sensation was her muscles groaning or her unexplained reaction when she was with him.

When she reached the women's locker room, he kept going but before she was out of earshot, he called over his shoulder. "By the way I have a proposition for you."

Talk about a heart skip. She dragged air into her lungs. "What kind of proposition?"

He motioned down the hallway. "I'll wait for you near the door." And he was gone.

Proposition. The word piqued her interest. While the shower splashed against her skin, easing her aches, nothing eased her mind. She stood in the spray, sorting through her foolish reaction to Jonny. If she'd met him on the street as a stranger, her resistance would have vanished, but their past relationship ruined that.

Her body humming with warmth and the apprehension of hearing Jonny's proposition, she turned off the water, toweled down and donned her street clothes. She ran a comb through her hair and peered at her unadorned face in the mirror. Usually after exercising she didn't bother with makeup, and even today, reality reminded her that Jonny had seen her looking worse than she did today, but the more she gazed at her drab face, the more the image of Jeannie Hunt's turned-up nose filled her mind.

Releasing a sigh, she drew out her makeup bag, brushed blush on her cheeks, dragged the mascara brush over her lashes, and guided lipstick over her mouth. She couldn't fool him with cosmetics, but at least she felt better. She dropped her towel and damp clothes into her duffle bag, then slipped her makeup and comb into the little zipper compartment and strode toward the exit.

Jonny smiled as she approached, and pushed open the outside door.

"Did you wait long?"

His eyes captured hers. "Seems like a lifetime."

The comment held a lilt of humor, but she sensed something deeper in his words. She walked beside him, her tight muscles sending messages to her brain that she'd overdone her exercise today, but she didn't care. She kept pace with Jonny's long legs, waiting to hear what he had to say.

"Which is your car?"

She pointed to her sport sedan, wondering if he'd forgotten about his proposition.

"Nice. I like the copper color." He strode beside her in silence.

When they reached her car, she hit the unlock button and gave up wondering. "I thought you had something you wanted to propose."

He rested his back against the side of her car. "Right. I do." He tucked his hands into his jacket pocket. "When we were talking about Rainie's engagement party, I meant to ask if you'd like me to pick you up. No sense in both of us driving."

Proposition had held more promise than the offer of a ride. "You don't have a date?"

"Me? No." His smile faded. "Unless you've already made plans."

"No plans. I thought I'd go alone."

His face darkened.

Her pulse skipped. "But I don't need to go alone. I'd be happy to have you pick me up if you don't mind."

"I don't mind at all." He gazed at her a moment, and then extended his hand.

She eyed it, realizing he was waiting for a shake. She slipped her hand in his, feeling the heat roll up her arm to her chest.

He squeezed her fingers, gave a faint nod and released her hand. "I should have asked the other day, but I know you were dealing with little Jonny the pest, and I didn't know if—"

"I'm sorry, Jonny. I don't mean to make such a big deal out of it, but those memories seem to stay in my mind." Along with the other dark ones she couldn't get rid of, either.

"It's okay, Neely. Maybe in time."

In time. Maybe. She studied his classic good looks, his dark hair with those crystal-blue eyes. Maybe one day she'd even remember to call him Jon.

Chapter Three

"Auntie."

Joey's squeal made Neely smile before she climbed from her sedan. She opened her arms as he leaped forward, and held him against her, his legs kicking in delight. The feel of her nephew's cheek against hers, the tightness of the two-year-old's arms, warmed her inside and out. "Where's your mama?"

"In." He swung his chunky arm toward the house, and she balanced his weight on her hip as she trudged to the screen door and pulled it open. "Ashley?"

Her sister darted into the kitchen, and when she saw Joey, surprise lit her face. "Was he outside?"

"Looks like it." She gave the toddler a bounce, and set him on the floor.

Ashley knelt in front of him and shook her head. "Joey. You can't go outside without Mama. You know that."

He pointed to the heavens. "Birdies."

She gave Neely a helpless look. "Yes, birdies, but ask Mama to go out with you, okay?"

Joey studied her a moment, as if he wanted to digest her request.

She shifted his chin so he faced her. "Do you want a time out?"

His head swung back and forth like a flag in the wind.

"Then you ask Mama so we can go outside together. Okay?"

"'kay." His decisive response rang with agreement. Apparently the time out did the trick.

Neely glowed, seeing again the intelligence of her nephew. His speech and abilities seemed ahead of his age. He had his daddy's smarts and his mama's loving ways.

Ashley shook her head, her expression wearing the look of defeat as Joey ran into the next room. "I don't know what I'm going to do with him. He's already a handful at two."

Neely chuckled "The terrible twos. But he's verging on three. Hopefully it won't be long." She wrapped her arm around her sister's shoulder, and guided her through the doorway where Joey had settled on the living room floor with a pile of blocks and miniature cars. "How are you?"

Ashley sank onto the sofa and motioned her to an easy chair. Moisture shone in her eyes and twisted Neely's heart. Almost two years had passed since Ashley's husband died for his country in the Middle East, but the pain of losing a soul mate couldn't be marked by years. The sorrow lasted a lifetime.

Her sister brushed away her tears. "Sorry, it still hits hard once in a while, especially days when Joey's antics are involved. I wish Adam could have known him, even for a little while."

Neely rose and settled beside her sister, grasping her hand. "Ash, he knew Joey. He knew him from the photos and all that you shared in your letters." Her words sounded empty. "You want more than that. I understand. But they'll meet one day, and what a glorious reunion they'll have."

Ashley rested her head on Neely's shoulder. "In heaven, you mean."

She could only nod, struggling to swallow the lump in her throat.

"You're right, sis." She raised her head followed by a ragged breath. "God gave me part of Adam when he blessed us with a son. I can be grateful for that, and for the time I had with Adam. I have to remember he died doing what he thought was right." She lowered her head with an easy wag. "Think of the many men and women who died in Afghanistan and left no children behind."

Her own lack of a family tinged her mind. "You're right, Ash. God gave you a wonderful gift." She motioned to Joey, absorbed with his cars and the block structure he'd devised. "And he's so bright. His hand-eye coordination is amazing."

Ashley smiled. "He takes after Adam."

Neely's purpose for stopping by became trivial in the midst of their conversation. She longed to say so many things that were brilliant and helpful, but she was lost. At this point in her life, she had no husband, no children, no way to deeply relate to her sister's sorrow.

Ashley's grieved expression smoothed away. "Let's talk about you. I haven't heard from you for a few days."

The reference to her absence made her feel enveloped in failure. She'd come home to spend time with her father and sister, but for the past few days her mind had been on running into Jonny and jolted by his reference to Erik. "I've been trying to get Dad settled. He needs to accept his condition and take better care of himself." Her excuse sounded feeble. A phone call took minutes.

"If anyone can do it, you can." Ashley nudged her. "Determination."

Neely grinned but didn't bother to respond since she had no rebuttal. Ashley's point was too true. "Another thing

I've done is started to exercise, and I've joined a gym." She gave her rounded hip a couple of pats. "I need to get back in shape." She gazed at her slender sister, aware that grief had taken off her pounds. "You remember my friend Lorraine Turner. Her brother Jonny told me about a new place called Tone and Trim Fitness Center. Remember him? He was such a pest?"

Ashley's chuckle lifted her spirit. "Not anymore, I bet. That was thirteen or fourteen years ago. Boys grow into men."

Jonny's image bolted into her mind, and warmth rolled up her neck. "Right. He's not a boy anymore. You should see him. If he weren't so young, and if I could forget the past, I'd be batting my eyes at him." A wince of reality shivered down her back. She probably had battered her eyes at him without wanting to.

"How much younger is he?"

"Four years." She shrugged, ignoring her escalating pulse. "He was such a—"

"Four years. That's nothing. The older you get age issues fade away. The guy's twenty-eight. If that's not a man, I don't know what is."

His tapered frame, broad shoulders trimming to a tight waist and long legs filled her mind. And those eyes.

Ashley shook her head as if Neely were an idiot. "I'm sure he's changed…besides looks, I mean?"

"Obviously. He's older. He makes me laugh. He's thoughtful. He showed concern about Dad and you, Ash. Very sincere. It touched me." The conversation hedged on danger. Ashley's expression already hinted at a comment brewing in her mind. "One thing for sure, I was impressed he doesn't hate me." She managed a grin. "You know he could with the way I treated him."

"So what's the downside of this guy?"

The question hung on the air. Downside? Her memory replayed their recent conversation, and she came up empty.

Ashley released a puff of air. “No downside?”

“I’m sure he has some.” Age, but Ashley already pooh-poohed that one. “I just can’t come up with any right now.” The reality of her answer threw her. “He’d be a catch for anyone.” Anyone but her. She couldn’t get past their previous relationship. But she couldn’t say it. Ashley had already negated that.

A fresh idea popped into her head. If Ashley were ready for a relationship, she would be blessed with Jonny as a husband. “Are you getting out at all, Ash?”

Her sister gave her a blank look.

“You need to socialize. How about a different job?” She loved the turn of the conversation. It got her sister off her back. “Maybe I should take care of Joey, and let you have a chance to meet some—”

“Stop.” Ashley’s hand flexed upward. “I’m working. I’m typing letters, addressing envelopes and creating some promotional materials for a few small businesses, and I can do that at home. Joey needs a parent, and I’m it.” She arched a brow. “And I suspect you have more on you mind than my socializing with women. Men? I don’t know, Neely. I’m waiting for that special someone.” Her gaze drifted out the window and the same gloom filled her face. “Adam and I had an amazing relationship. I won’t settle for anything less.”

“You’ll never know until you give someone a chance, Ash. You’re pushing me to find a relationship, and yet you’re—”

“It’ll happen.” Ashley’s gaze penetrated hers. “But it has to be natural. It’s something that can’t be planned.” She shook her head, the hint of a grin on her lips. “No blind dates.”

With her matchmaking efforts thwarted, Neely dropped the subject. "Speaking of men. I didn't tell you everything."

"Everything about Jonny?

"No, Erik."

Ashley drew back. "Erik. You mean 'the' Erik. I thought that ended long ago."

"It did, and that's how I want it."

Ashley's expression fell askew. "Is there a problem? Why is he an issue now?"

"Jonny told me he would be at Rainie's engagement party. I didn't realize Erik was still in town." Her skin prickled with memories. "I want to steer clear of him. How can I do that now?"

Ashley's brow arched. "Say hi and walk away. It's no big deal, Neely. Find a date. Do you know anyone who would—"

"Jonny told me he'd be happy to drive me there." She brightened as a new idea struck her. "Maybe he can pretend that I'm his date." The possibility dampened, and she faltered. "But I'm not sure that would make a difference with Erik. He knows how to add pressure."

Memories spewed in her mind. His persistence to prove her love had been unending until she'd given in, and he didn't stop there. When he managed to get her somewhere alone, he'd laugh if she said no. "What difference does it make now," he'd ask, and he'd knock down every reason she named. Giving in had been a horrible mistake. After that experience she felt as if the men she'd dated had the same motive in mind, and that's why she'd decided sticking to God's will was her answer.

Instead of smiling, Ashley sat in silence, a frown growing on her face. "Did I hear you right? You want to use Jonny?"

"It's not exactly using him." Her pulse kicked. "He offered to pick me up and—"

"He offered a ride." Ash shook her head. "You treated him awfully when he was a kid, and now you plan to use him for your purpose again. You're using him as a battering ram."

She winced at her sister's comment. Though Ashley didn't know about her intimacy with Erik, she'd expected her to understand why she wanted to hide behind Jonny's presence.

"How does Jonny feel about this?" Ashley's thoughtful look unsettled her.

Neely swallowed, already knowing what her sister would say. "I didn't explain it to him yet."

"You think he'll want to be your pawn. You think he's not good enough for a real date." Ashley drew in a lengthy breath while Neely waited for her to continue. "I see."

She didn't, and she never would understand until Neely told her the truth about letting Erik take advantage of her, and her pride wouldn't do that.

"He's four years younger than me. He poured sand in my hair when he was a kid. I'm not going to date him for real. And I'm not playing a game with him." Neely held her breath.

"You don't think so?" A grim look slipped over her face. "It's more than that, Neely. It's something I've noticed and—"

"More than what? I don't know what you're talking about." Ashley's expression made her uneasy.

"You remind me of Mother."

Neely's head jerked back. "Mother? Never." Ice ran through her veins. "Why would you say that?"

"Do you recall problems you had with Mom?" She gave her head a sharp shake. "That *we* had?"

"She was self-focused." But that wasn't all, and Ashley knew it.

"And critical. No matter how hard Daddy tried to please her, he didn't do it the right way. He didn't say the right thing. He didn't wear the right tie. He didn't drive slow enough or fast enough."

The words bit through Neely's defense, but she toughened her guard. "I'm not critical like Mom. Not at all."

"It's not identical, but you find fault with people when you become vulnerable."

She opened her mouth to rebut, but Ashley flexed her palm.

"Don't stop me, sis. I'm saying this because I love you."

Neely had heard it before. She could hear her mother's nitpicking voice ring in her ears. "What are you talking about? How am I vulnerable?"

"When Erik got too close, you backed away, looking for greener grass as they say. You thought maybe the future held something better."

"And it did." Her voice split the air, and Joey let out a whimper. She winced at her lack of control.

"Maybe so, but you walked in here and told me how Jonny was kind and good-looking and someone you could be interested in, but then you attacked his age." Ashley looked heavenward and shook her head. "His age? Is that not stupid? I wouldn't have cared if Adam had been six years younger than me. I noticed him first for his looks, but I fell in love with him for his wonderful qualities. You need to value people for what's important."

Neely cringed. She'd made a mistake talking with Ashley about anything related to men. She'd lost her husband, and that had skewed her attitude.

Ashley rose and lifted Joey in her arms, giving him

a hug. He eyed her a moment, and then squirmed down toward the floor. She settled him back amid the cars and blocks, and then dug into his toy box for a couple new distractions.

Looking at two people she loved, Neely felt an ache in her chest. Why had Ashley thrown their mother in her face? Her sister knew her motivation for leaving town was her mother's constant criticism, and she'd just grown more determined to get away. And while duty had motivated her homecoming, once she'd arrived, love and hope overpowered her need to make retribution for her absence.

"I know you're being like a big sister, Ash, but you're confusing me. Why do you say I didn't find something better? I had a good job—"

"Wait a minute. You walked away from your life in Indianapolis. If it was so great, why would you leave your apartment, your friends, and more job opportunities than you'll find here in Michigan. Positions aren't easy to come by." Instead of returning to the sofa, she sank into an easy chair. "Now you're worried about Erik, and that doesn't make sense. Brush him off. If you're not interested in Jonny, don't lead him on for your own purpose. Jonny sounds like a nice guy, and maybe someone who could make you happy, but you won't give him a chance. Or any guy for that matter, it seems. When I fell in love with Adam, I married him for better or worse, sis. I didn't expect worse, but it happened. Still, I wouldn't give up one moment of our time together and the love we shared." Her gaze drifted to Joey.

Ashley's words jolted her. "Maybe I wasn't in love with Erik, but I thought I was. I certainly never loved Jonny although I will admit as much as I bad-mouthed him, I found his attentiveness cute. I don't want to hurt Jonny now. I planned to be honest with him. No games."

"There's no harm, I suppose, if you're honest and he

agrees." She closed her eyes with the look of exasperation. "But you've told me he's a great guy. Don't slough him off. See where your friendship goes." She rested her hands on her knees, and leaned forward. "Real love is wonderful, Neely. I want love to find me again. No one will ever replace Adam, but I miss feeling complete. Part of me feels empty as if something is missing. I want to feel whole again, but it will take someone special."

Drawing her shoulders back, Ashley straightened. "I want you to know that kind of love. When you described Jonny, I sensed that he could be a special person, and for once in your life, you couldn't find one thing wrong with him." She gave Neely a pointed look. "Except he's a couple years younger."

"Four."

Ashley rolled her eyes. "Four years. Open your eyes to opportunities, Neely. Mom criticized her way through life never really seeing the man who loved her so much."

"Dad." The word caught in her throat.

"He forgave her…always, and he tolerated her constant badgering not because he wasn't strong, but because he loved her. Love is a power beyond understanding. When you find it, it will glue itself to your thoughts and your heart."

"Maybe, Ash, but I don't know if I will ever feel that kind of love."

Her sister grinned. "One of these days, I'll be able to say 'I told you so.'" She rose and settled beside Neely. "My advice, sis, is keep your eyes and heart open, and love will find you, and then knock your socks off."

Ashley grinned and opened her arms while Neely molded into her embrace. If anyone knew about love, it was Ashley.

Chapter Four

Neely looked out her bedroom window, anticipating Jonny's arrival to take her to Rainie and Ty's engagement party. She wished she would have talked with him first about pretending she was his date. She'd never had a chance, and when she saw him at the gym, others were around and it didn't seem the right place.

The more she planned to ask him, the more her sister's comments stopped her. Using him as a battering ram—her sister's words—made her flinch, and though she thought Ashley's analogy was a poor one, she still got the idea. She wanted to use him as a buffer between her and Erik. The problem might not arise, but if so, she hoped Jonny would understand.

How did she expect anyone to understand without knowing the details? The question nudged her so often, but being honest about the situation meant soiling her reputation and making her vulnerable. She couldn't handle that.

She checked her dress in the long mirror. The A-line style in deep teal hung in soft folds and camouflaged her less-than-perfect figure, although she'd already lost a few pounds at the gym. She'd come home to be a support to her dad and sister, but she faced her other motive. She wanted to remake herself as well as her body. Though she disagreed with Ashley again on being like her mother, she had to admit that she did tend to run from problems. Her issues with Erik and her mother had been prime examples, but now she'd returned and had to deal with the same conflict unless Erik had changed. She could only hope.

The doorbell rang, and she looked down from the upper window. Jonny's car had rolled into the driveway while she'd been preoccupied. Her dad's voice sounded from the foyer, followed by Jonny's greeting. She grasped her small handbag and hurried down the steps. Before she reached the bottom, she faltered, her heartbeat skipping as she eyed Jonny in a dark-colored suit with a white shirt and conservative dark tie.

He took her breath away. She hadn't realized the width of his shoulders until now. As she opened her mouth to compliment him, Jonny cut her off with his own comment.

"You look beautiful, Neely." He reached for her hand as she left the last step, and squeezed her fingers. "I'll bring her home safe and sound, Mr. Andrews."

Her father chuckled, and rested his hand on Jonny's shoulder. "I know I can trust you, Jon. You're a good man."

She grinned at her dad, agreeing that Jonny had grown into a wonderful man. The more the truth hit her the worse she felt using him as protection. She hoped it didn't come to that.

"Daddy, I want you to stay downstairs until I get back. You have everything you need down here, and when I get home, I'll be with you when you walk upstairs."

Her father shook his head as if she were a blithering idiot. "What can I do with this girl, Jon? She thinks I'm an invalid."

"She loves you, Mr. Andrews."

She grinned at Jonny who'd backed toward the door, grateful he hadn't agreed that she'd been overreacting. She drew closer and kissed her father's cheek. "Do as I say, Daddy, and I'll be home no later than midnight—probably earlier." She eyed Jonny for validation, but he only grinned.

"Good night, sir." He turned the knob, and pulled the door open, then held it for her to step outside.

Neely gave a final wave at her dad standing in the doorway as he'd done when she was a teenager. She grinned, thinking about those years when she felt protected and supported. This time it was her turn to protect her father, a kind of reversal of roles she'd never anticipated but one she accepted.

Jonny opened the passenger door of his car, and she slipped inside, admiring his tall frame as he rounded the hood to the driver side. When he settled beside her, a woodsy scent enveloped her, and she drew it in, admiring the man who wore it.

"Your dad looks pretty good." He started the car, and shifted into Reverse.

"You should have seen him a few weeks ago." She shook her head with the memory. "I think it was the fear in his eyes that bothered me the most. I've never seen Daddy vulnerable, but that's exactly what he was."

"Severe illnesses remind us of our finite nature." He guided the car onto the street and pulled away. "Heart attacks, accidents, diseases can attack us at any time. Even when we're fit."

She agreed, sorry that the topic came up. No one wanted to think of life ending so soon. But it did, and that meant each person had to be ready. She closed her eyes, wishing she didn't feel the weight of her sins.

"Speaking of fit."

Jonny's voice drew her back. "You're looking great,

Neely. I've noticed the weight you lost although you've always looked good."

She grinned, using his compliment to give a lift to her spirit. "Thanks, but that would be in the eye of the beholder, as they say. I behold pounds."

"You're too hard on yourself."

Maybe she was.

"If the weather stays this nice, we should take advantage it and enjoy the outdoors. Wilson Park has an in-line skating rink. I use it sometimes for running."

"Fresh air and sunshine. Sounds good."

"Next week. I'll call you."

She nodded, asking herself why she had gotten herself so involved in Jonny. She needed motivation to exercise and doing it with someone added fun to the job, but Jonny? Sometimes she thought of herself as a fly caught in a spider web and tempting fate. She gazed at him again, and grinned. Jonny was the best-looking web weaver she'd ever run into.

When they reached the steak house, Jonny slipped from behind the wheel and was at her door before she could unhook her seat belt. When she stepped onto the asphalt, he closed and locked the door, and clasped her arm as they headed to the entrance. Though he had no idea that she'd considered asking him to pretend the outing was a date, he gave the illusion with his attentiveness. Grateful she hadn't asked, she accepted the attention as they went inside.

The maître d' guided them to the banquet room, and when they stepped inside, a good feeling washed over her. She and Rainie had dreamed of the day when they would walk down the aisle, each promising to ask the other to be their maid or matron of honor. In a few months, she would fulfill her part of the promise. Rainie's part of the promise seemed like a faraway dream.

"Neely." Rainie stood with a group of women and waved her over.

She slipped her arm from Jonny's grasp. "Your sister calls."

He gave a nod, and headed for Ty without looking back.

She stood a moment to watch him cross the room, part of her wondering how it might be to really be on a date with Jonny.

When she turned toward Rainie, someone caught her arm. Glancing over her shoulder, she cringed and then pulled herself together before facing him. "Erik, how are you?"

"Neely." He stared at her, his jaw loose as if it had a broken hinge. "Wow! You're the last person in the world I expected to run into."

His gaze swept over her, and her discomfort increased. Words were lost in the jumble of thoughts running through her head. He'd grown more handsome. His boyish features had matured and strengthened. His sandy-colored hair had darkened to saddle brown, worn in a typical executive style with a fresh-cut look. He wore a sport coat with his shirt open at the neck and had the air of a man who'd just come from a business meeting.

Erik's eyes searched hers. "You look healthy."

Did he mean fat? Flushed? She probably was. Her face burned, as their past reeled into her mind. "Thanks. You look well, too, Erik." Though her pulse raged, she managed to keep an even tone. Why did he have to approach her when she was alone?

A waitress shifted beside Erik with a tray. "Would you like a drink?"

Erik grasped a wineglass while she eyed the tray for a soft drink. "Is that cola?"

"It is." The woman smiled and handed her the glass, then moved away to offer drinks to other guests.

Neely watched her go, wishing the woman would stay and chat. She scanned the guests hoping to catch Jonny's attention but he'd vanished. She wished Erik would. She sipped her drink before focusing on him.

He swirled the red wine in the stemware, and sniffed the scent before he spoke. "Sorry about your dad. I heard he had quite a time."

Surprised he'd mentioned her father, she took a second to respond. "Thanks. His health is one reason I came home. I knew he'd need watching, and Ashley has her hands full."

"Yes, I heard about your sister's loss, too." He rested his hand on hers. "So you're here to stay?"

"That depends." She pressed her lips together and stepped back, hoping he'd withdraw his hand. He didn't.

A grin stole to his mouth. "Depends on what?"

"On my dad's health and the job market."

His gaze slipped to her left hand. "You're still single?"

Her chest constricted, and a response clung to her throat. Finally she found her words. "Yes, and very happy about that."

"Really?" His head flew back so hard, she feared he gave himself a whiplash. "I always pictured you with the country-club crowd. Remember our plans."

"Country club? I don't think so. The lady said she's happy."

Jonny's voice rolled through her, and she sent a thank-you to heaven. "Jonny, where have you been?"

"I was trapped by a football fan." He shifted his attention to Erik. "How's business?" Jonny's question salved the uncomfortable situation, and she relaxed, grateful he'd come to her rescue.

She listened to them talk about their work while her

mind weighed the burden of having Erik come back into her life. She'd hoped he'd moved away to a big city somewhere. At the moment, she wanted to move away from him. She scanned the room until she spotted Rainie, remembering she'd flagged her down minutes earlier. She had her excuse to say goodbye, and leave the men with their conversation.

While she waited for a break to cut in, Jonny slipped his arm around her waist, and gave her a gorgeous smile. Her heart flew to her throat. She hadn't asked him to protect her, but that's what he was doing.

Erik didn't miss the move. His face flickered with question as tension tightened his jaw. "What are you two doing together?"

She had no idea what to say, and searched Jonny's face waiting for him to reply, but he didn't. He only grinned.

Neely grinned, too, waiting.

Erik's gaze dropped to Jonny's arm around her waist, and when he looked up, he managed a chuckle tinged with sarcasm. "I assume you've let bygones be bygones."

Jonny arched his brow. "We're not kids anymore, Erik. We put childish behaviors behind us."

Neely wondered if Erik recognized the scripture reference. He'd never talked about faith. She was a believer, and she cringed again, knowing that she'd allowed him to manipulate her into ignoring her morals and upbringing for his pleasure.

Erik appeared to have gotten grip of his emotions. He gave her a wink, and lifted his wineglass. "It's good to see you again, Neely. Let's toast a new beginning."

She studied him wanting to walk away, but this wasn't the time for a confrontation. She lifted her soda glass while Erik held his drink posed until Jonny joined the toast. They clinked their glasses together, and when Erik lowered his, he captured her gaze with a coy grin. "I'll let you two enjoy yourselves, and, Neely, tell your sister I'm sorry about her loss. She's way too attractive to be alone, isn't she? That's too bad."

His comment seemed a little glib. She flinched as he turned away, but Jonny's hold on her waist soothed her, and when she turned her focus to him, the sight of his beautiful eyes washed away the tension.

Jonny chucked her chin. "That's over. Let's have some fun."

She tiptoed up, and kissed his cheek. "Thank you."

As they walked toward Rainie, Jonny almost gave the impression that this was a date, and she didn't care. His protective nature nestled around her, and tonight she tried to forget the old Jonny. As Erik had said, she would toast a new Jonny and a new beginning.

Jon listened to girl talk between his sister and Neely for a few minutes, and then ambled away, unnoticed. He stood closer to the hall entrance and surveyed the crowd, seeing a few high school friends of Rainie's but also people he really didn't know. He spotted Erik who seemed to be charming a young woman Jon didn't recognize. He wondered if Neely fell for the new-beginning toast. He wanted to gag, but what right did he have to interfere? Dreams didn't count in the scheme of things. To be a winner meant developing a game plan by setting up plays, and then moving into action. He taught his boys how to play on the field, and now he wondered if the same skills could be used in relationships.

The whole situation plagued him. The best parts of the evening were Neely's kiss on his check and Erik's expression when he slipped his arm around Neely's waist. He would have never had the courage except he knew she wanted nothing to do with Erik. He figured a flash of possession might thwart his obvious plans to hook Neely back into his arms.

He still wasn't sure what caused her to be turned off by Erik, but whatever it was, he was glad.

An appetizer table he hadn't noticed earlier appeared, and he wandered closer, eyeing the tidbits of food that were on the menu. Shrimp, cheeses, crackers, a series of chaffing dishes that promised tiny kabobs of meat, mushrooms with filling, and some he couldn't make out, but the scent of herbs and spices rose from the table. He forked a couple of unknowns on the plate and carried it and his soft drink to a small empty table.

He savored one of the mystery items, thinking he'd go back and try another—maybe even learn its name, and as he reached for a meatball in sauce, a hand swept a sausage wrapped in a dough from his plate. He recognized the bracelet and grinned. "You're welcome, Neely."

She settled into the chair beside him, and took a bite of the appetizer. "Yummy." She licked her lips, and then slipped his napkin from beneath the plate to wipe her fingers. "Thanks." She motioned to the table. "I suppose I could get my own."

"Here, finish mine." He slid the plate in front of her. "I'll load up another plate for both of us."

She chuckled and delved into the stuffed mushroom. He hurried back and selected hors d'oeuvres for two plates, checked to make sure Erik was still preoccupied and carried the dishes back to the table. Erik's country-club comment bothered him. He didn't understand how that reference had entered the conversation. Neely had never seemed interested in all of that.

He set the plates on the table and returned to his chair. "What was that reference to country-club crowd?"

She drew in a deep breath and shook her head. “That was one of Erik’s encouragers.”

“Encouragers?” He let the word bounce in his mind. “Encouragers for what?”

“For a girl to be his wife. He thought everyone valued having membership in a country club. That was far from my mind.”

He chuckled. “Very far. You were down to earth. Always giving.”

“Me?” A grin brightened her face. “Look what you just did. You gave me your plate, and then went to fill two more. I don’t know why I’m surprised, I remember, as much as you irked me year ago, you were always thoughtful. Helpful, really.”

“So were you. You’ve always focused on the needs of others. I’ve seen you give a needy woman a piece of clothing you were wearing.”

Her eyes capture his. “I what?” She shook her head. “I don’t remember that? “

Maybe he’d admitted too much. “I helped you and Rainie take the canned goods you’d collected to a food kitchen in Detroit somewhere. It was October. I remember there was a chilly breeze, and…” He caught himself again, letting his sentence fade.

“October? Come on. How would you remember that?”

Her eyes grew as large as the pumpkin on her shirt that day. He’d done it. Too much information. He might as well tell her he could remember everything she wore back then. “When you gave the woman your sweater, underneath you were wearing a knit shirt that had a big pumpkin on it, and—”

“Jonny, I can’t believe you remembered that crazy pumpkin top.” Her gaping mouth drew into a smile. “I think I blocked that gaudy thing from my memory.”

But he hadn't. When she'd hoisted the carton of food from the trunk, the sunlight hit her auburn hair and streaked it with gold, the color of leaves at the height of autumn. It had taken his breath away. He'd just turned fourteen, and Neely had become his first secret love.

Neely shook her head as a soft chuckle escaped her. "Why would you remember something like that?"

Talk about reality, the truth smacked him in the head. "Because I had the biggest crush on you."

Her hand flew up, and flipped the edge of the plate. Two appetizers skipped to the table. She dropped them back on the plate, though her eyes never left him. "What are you saying? You had a crush on me?" She burst into a laugh. "You were a pesky kid."

To her maybe, but to him, he was a man in love.

She lifted her hand and pressed his arm. "I'm sorry. I'm sure, at the time, you thought you were in love. I guess I did that, too. I remember picturing me in the arms of Leonardo DiCaprio." She lifted her brows. "Sometimes I can still picture that."

A faint chuckle tittered from her as if she were a teenager again.

She broke eye contact and smiled. "So you had a crush on me."

Not *had—have.* He managed to return the grin as he picked up his drink. His tongue adhered to the roof of his mouth as if he'd eaten glue. She'd already taken his confession as a joke, and he needed to let it go for now. In time, he hoped she would see who he was from his actions. A man's actions had to mean more than his age. He gazed at her, his mind going back. "Another thing I remember."

"You remember more?"

"Not really." He let it drop. He'd said too much already.

"Want to mingle?" He started to rise but she grabbed the hem of his jacket and tugged.

"No, I want to know what you remember."

Her lighthearted tone urged him on, and though he knew he could be digging his own demise, he decided to be open. He could be Jonny for now if that's what it took. "The country-club comment reminded me of this."

She frowned at first before brightening again. "Go ahead."

"I remember once you said, 'Who needs sterling silver and fine china. I like paper plates and plastic forks. No dishes to wash.' You wrinkled your nose and laughed. I remember."

"Were you memorizing my conversations with your sister?" She arched an eyebrow, and he couldn't tell if she were teasing or upset.

"Crushes do that. Can't you remember everything about Leonardo DiCaprio's face when he stood on the bow of the *Titanic* with Kate Winslet?"

Her expression turned to a grin. "I guess you're right." She reached over, and rested her hand on his again. "I think we should mingle, but first, I want to thank you again for coming to my aid with Erik. He really bothers me."

Her expression validated what she'd said. Erik ground him, too. "What was that comment about Ashley?"

"That's what I'd like to know." This time she did frown.

So did he, because he could only guess that Ashley could become the pawn of another of Erik's manipulations to get what he wanted.

He didn't like it at all.

Chapter Five

Neely opened the back door and stopped, seeing her father with his nose in the refrigerator. She eyed the clock. "It's a little early for dinner, Dad. Are you hungry?"

"Can't I eat a snack if I want to?"

His head remained behind the fridge door, and when he straightened, he backed away with a hunk of cheese and piece of ham. "I thought I'd have a sandwich."

The clock read three-thirty. Neely shook her head. "Then that will be your dinner, I guess."

"Dinner? I said it's a snack."

She jammed her fists into her waist. "A snack is an apple or a cookie, not a sandwich. That's dinner."

"Who said?" He ignored her by facing the counter as he built a sandwich.

"Your doctor. He said you needed to eat healthy and take off a little weight."

Her dad waved his hand over his shoulder. "Pooh. What does he know?"

Her shoulders slumped. "You frustrate me, Dad." She walked to his side, and touched his arm. "I don't want to see you sick again. You need to take care of yourself."

He gave her a half glance. "I am. I'm making a sandwich."

Her hand slipped from his arm, and she shook her head. "Fine." She headed toward the doorway, and then paused. Having a tiff with her dad would serve no purpose. "I had a nice visit with Ashley. We talked about going out to dinner tonight. Want to join us?"

"No. I'm happy at home."

That was his problem. Since her mother died, he had lost motivation to live. He ate wrong, got no exercise, and stared at the TV. But his determination was stronger than hers and getting him to make changes seemed hopeless. She needed someone to prompt him to alter his choices, but it had to be someone he'd listen to. Apparently that person wasn't her.

"Would you like to take a ride to Ash's to see Joey? He's getting cuter every day."

He took a bite of his sandwich, and didn't respond.

She guessed his answer. No. Not even Joey excited him. Though she didn't want to stir up trouble, she knew she had to do something. "Dad."

The telephone's ring stopped her. Maybe it was for the best. She crossed the room and grabbed the receiver. Jonny's voice caught her by surprise.

"How about running at the park today? You can't count on another September day being so warm."

Neely glanced at her father and figured he'd be glad to get rid of her for a couple of hours.

"What time?"

"I'll pick you up at four.

"That works. I'll be ready." But she detested the excitement she felt.

"How about dinner afterward?"

Her pulse did a double flip, and then she remembered. "I

made plans to eat out with Ashley, but you'd be welcome. She'd love to see you." And maybe this could be the beginning of something wonderful for her sister, and that way, her pulse would tick at a normal rate. She'd never mess around with her sister's boyfriend.

"Are you positive?"

She chuckled. "Yes, and you could meet Joey, too. He's a charmer."

"If you're sure."

She assured him, and then hung up. "I'm going for a run at Wilson Park, Dad, but I'll be home to change before dinner. Think about it, please. Dinner with Ash and Joey would get you out of this house."

He shook his head, and brushed her words away. "Stop worrying about me. You're worse than your mother." He grinned. "Besides, I already had dinner, remember?"

Neely braced her hands on her knees and caught her breath. Her legs burned from running, but the fresh air and sunshine made it worthwhile. She tilted her head upward and looked at Jonny who didn't seem to be winded at all. "How many times did we run around the in-line skating track?"

"Too many." He motioned toward the car. "We can walk to the car from here—no more running.

She chuckled at his playful comment, still rattled by her good feeling with him. "I had a great time today."

"So did I. We can do this anytime." He rested his hand on her shoulder. "You're glowing, you know."

"Do you mean sweat or a red face?"

He leaned back and laughed. "A real glow, healthy pink cheeks."

The way he looked at her sent her pulse charging up her arm, and she cautioned her wayward thoughts. Ogling

Rainie's younger brother made no sense. She would be a cradle snatcher. And worse yet, how could she tell him the truth about her relationship with Erik? She couldn't get involved with that mistake between them. He deserved a pure, wholesome wife. Jonny would always be…Jonny.

Though she told herself it was for the best, part of her fought the reality. She jerked her mind back to her resent plan. Jonny and Ashley. "What did you have in mind for dinner? I like to get my thoughts primed."

He chucked and shrugged. "It's your pick. Howe's Bayou has a mean po'boy."

"Crispy French bread filled with meat or fish." She shook her head and grinned. "Fatten me up, will you?"

He slipped his arm around her shoulder, and squeezed. "Okay no po'boy. They have salads."

"Is it quiet there? Good for talking?"

He drew back and eyed her. "I thought we were eating."

She'd bungled. He and Ashley needed time to get to know each other if anything might happen, but playing matchmaker was against Ashley's wishes and probably not on Jonny's agenda, either. She faced it. The matchmaking idea had become her own self-defense against her crazy emotions. "I suppose you're right." She managed a playful expression. "Can we stop by and pick up Ashley on the way back to my house?" Then he could drop her off home after dinner. Her plan had taken a turn, but a good one.

He nodded, his mind seemingly focused on something else.

She pulled out her cell phone to warn Ashley of the new plan and to her surprise, Jonny headed in the right direction, as if he knew where Ashley lived. When he turned down the street, she pointed, but he'd already aimed the nose the car into the driveway. A frown tugged at her forehead but she managed to grin it away. Why he knew where Ashley lived was none of her business, and except for the tug of her heart, it didn't matter.

Before she could step outside, Ashley waved from the doorway, and Jonny hurried from the car and headed toward the porch. When Ashley appeared with Joey, Jonny grasped the car seat and Joey's hand while Ashley carried the diaper bag and another tote.

Neely's chest tightened seeing him grinning at Joey who was carrying on a conversation as if he'd known Jonny forever. Watching the scene warmed around her heart. Maybe her matchmaking idea had been part of God's plan. Jonny would make a great father.

Ashley opened the back door and tossed in the bags. "This worked out well. Can you believe Dad called and offered to watch Joey while we go to dinner?"

Neely's head jerked toward her. "That is news." Her father's "stop worrying about me. You're worse than your mother" softened. Her dad wanted it to be his idea and not hers. She had to learn to hint and not suggest. Two determined minds could make a positive after all. "I'm glad he suggested it. Dad needs to find a purpose again, Ash. He doesn't have Mom prodding him, and when I do, he resents it."

"It's a learning curve, I suppose."

Jonny had shifted Ashley out of the way and attached the car seat. He hooked Joey in while Ashley rounded the car, and slipped in the other side.

Jonny gave a final tug on the seat belts. "You look safe enough, buddy." He gave Joey a grin, and closed the door.

Neely sat with her heart in her throat. She'd love to see Ashley find a man like Jonny, but a sense of possession sneaked into her thoughts. Jonny had brightened her world lately, and how would she handle it if he and Ashley did connect? She drew in a breath. She'd set this up and she would have to deal with it.

Jon glanced into the rearview mirror, his focus on Joey. His heart broke for a child who'd never known his father. He'd learned so much from his dad when he was growing up. Support, guidance and love. All three made him who he was today. Not perfect maybe, but striving to be all he could be with God's help.

If Ashley were as strong as Neely, she would not only survive but she would grow even stronger. That's what Neely had done. He admired both women, but his gaze lingered on Neely. He listened to the sister's talk, mainly about their dad, and he empathized with them. Their father had gone through a frightening experience, and that had affected his outlook on life. With his wife gone—from what he knew, a rather demanding wife—no wonder the man felt lost.

He'd witnessed Neely's frustration, and he wished he could make a difference in the man's life. His own parents were still healthy and active, and they didn't need his help at all. One day they would, but for now he thanked the Lord that they lived well. He should see them more often. A flash of guilt zipped through his chest. He could at least call more often. They lived so close, dropping by for a moment should be a no-brainer.

He pulled into Neely's driveway, and helped Ashley with Joey's car seat, then said goodbye with plans to pick them up in a half hour. When he pulled away, he spotted Neely holding open the front door while Ashley maneuvered Joey and the car seat through the entrance, but Neely's eyes were on him. His stomach tightened with the awareness. He gave a last wave and pulled away.

Though he'd agreed to join the sisters for dinner, he'd

been disappointed. He longed to spend time with Neely while she got to know him as Jon, a man who had a lot to offer her if she'd let him. He'd lived that dream since she'd walked back into his life. He sighed, wondering what God had in store for him. He hoped and prayed he wouldn't be hurt if the outcome wasn't as he wished.

He took only minutes hopping into the shower and dressing. He slipped on navy pants with a blue and gray shirt open at the neck and a gray sport coat, ran a comb through his hair and hurried back to his car. His parents stayed in his mind, and if he had time, he would drop in to say hello, but he didn't want to keep two beautiful women waiting for him.

A smile broke on his face thinking of Joey. The young boy—not even three—talked to him as if they were best friends. His experience with kids was limited, but he'd found the boy intriguing—bright and curious with a gift for gab at that young age.

Within minutes he pulled into Neely's driveway. Should he wait or go to the door? He chose the latter. The door opened and Mr. Andrews pushed it wide and waved him in. "Nice to see you again, Jon."

He stood a moment not sure if he should take a seat or wait.

Neely's father beckoned him toward the kitchen. When he came through the doorway, her dad had crossed to a pan on the stove and stirred what looked like macaroni and cheese. Farther down the counter, a box validated his guess. "You can't beat this for dinner."

Mr. Andrews grinned, and pointed to Joey who'd just sneaked in behind him. "My grandson's a fan of mac and cheese. Aren't you, boy?"

Joey nodded, a grin spreading on his face. "Me 'n' Papa eat mac 'n' cheese."

An old wooden high chair sat in the corner, and Neely's dad dragged it to the table. He hoisted Joey into the chair and placed their dinner onto two plates. He turned. "Somehow you got stuck with both my girls, I hear."

Jon chuckled, and gave a nod. "Guess I have, but I wouldn't call it stuck. It's sort of a privilege."

He arched an eyebrow. "You think so. Hmm?"

"I have an advantage. They don't try to tell me what to do."

Her dad slapped his leg, and let out a guffaw. "You can say that again." He motioned to the chair. "Have a seat."

Though he felt uncomfortable interfering with their dinner, Jon pulled out a chair and sat. Joey dug into his mac and cheese, manipulating his small-sized fork like a professional. When he turned, Neely's father was staring at him.

"What's your interest in my daughters?"

Huh? The question stumped him. "I'm friends with Neely."

He arched his brow. "And that's it?"

So far, but he wanted so much more. He gave a casual nod, and her father did the same.

The sound of footsteps ended the awkward moment. He looked toward the doorway, and watched Neely follow Ashley into the kitchen.

Ashley walked past him to Joey, but Neely stopped and leaned against the door jamb. "Sorry. I decided to take a shower."

So had he, but he knew women took longer to get dressed. He gave a shrug. "No problem. Your dad and I were talking." He hoped she didn't ask about what. "Are you ready?"

She gave a nod, but Ashley paused. "Where are we

going, Jon? I want my dad to know just in case." She tilted her head toward Joey.

So much for the surprise. "I thought we'd go to Assaggi Bistro."

Neely gave him a questioning look. "I thought you said Howe's Bayou."

He gave her a wink. "This is better."

Ashley turned to Fred. "Did you hear, Dad? We'll be at Assaggi Bistro if you need me."

Fred gave Ashley one of his looks. "You think I'm deaf?"

Jon grinned, but Ashley ignored him. She leaned over and kissed Joey's cheek. "Mama will be back in a little while, big boy."

Joey held up his fork. "Mac 'n' cheese, Mama."

"Yummy." Ashley tousled his hair before following Neely to the front door.

"Good night, sir. I'll take good care of your daughters."

"You'd better." He grinned and waved him off. Jon made a quick getaway, uncertain at times how to take their father's sense of humor.

The trip to the restaurant took minutes, and when it came into view, he slowed and found access to parking. He turned off the ignition and gave her a wink. "Have you been here?"

"No, but—"

"Good. It's fun to introduce you to new restaurants." He could see she had something on her mind, and guessed what it was. "Dinner's my treat."

When she opened her mouth, he gave her a look that closed it. He loved seeing her befuddled. Rarely did Neely give in, but he assumed she didn't want to embarrass her sister, since he interpreted her money comment as worrying about her sister's income.

Inside, the maître d' approached, and Jon pointed to their options. "Would you like to eat on the patio or inside?"

Neely looked at Ashley, and she only shrugged, so Neely turned back to him. "The weather's great. Outside would be nice."

He agreed, and they were guided onto the flagstone patio and seated near the stone fountain. The water trickled into the basin and the sound gave him a sense of Tuscany. Lighting strung around the periphery defined the boundaries and plants added to the ambience. He wished the evening had been only with Neely, but her sister deserved some time away from home, too, so he reminded himself to be grateful for the opportunity to enjoy a good dinner with two attractive women.

"This is lovely." Neely gazed at the decor before checking the menu.

"Let's start with an antipasto plate. Sound good?" He eyed the two women. They both nodded, and when the waiter arrived, he put in the order along with three iced teas.

Ashley gave him a direct look. "Thanks for being so good with Joey."

"How could I not? He's a charmer and so bright."

She lowered her eyes. "He's so much like his daddy."

His stomach knotted with the look on her face, and a response sailed off on the breeze. He looked at Neely before making his mouth work. "I can't imagine how hard it's been."

Her shoulder lifted in a weak shrug. "It's part of life, I suppose. I'm blessed with Joey."

"You sure are." He released air from his lungs, grateful when the waiter arrived with the appetizer and drinks. Neely and Ashley delved into the meats, imported cheeses along with artichokes and olives. He waited, wondering if they wanted to say a blessing. They seemed to notice his hesitation, and folded their hands. He offered a quiet praise for their time together and for the food, and then they dug in.

After a few bites, Ashley rummaged in into her purse and pulled out her cell phone. "Sorry. I forget to tell Dad where I put Joey's bag with his toys and pajamas." She held up a finger and left the table.

He grinned at Neely. "I don't think Ashley's comfortable with babysitters."

"I think Dad's been the first sitter so she's nervous." She gave him a playful jab. "But then what do you know. You're not a dad yet."

Yet. The idea fluttered through him. One day he hoped to be a husband and father. His gaze shifted to Neely as his chest constricted. One day.

Ashley returned, looking more assured. And the waiter arrived to take their dinner orders, two hand-rolled pasta Bolognese and his Angus flatiron steak. He couldn't pass up their beef. Before he refocused on his appetizer, he heard a familiar voice and lost his appetite.

"Now this is a surprise. Jon with two lovely women."

Erik's comment startled both women from their expressions, especially Neely.

Without being asked, Erik pulled out the fourth chair. "Do you mind?"

Jon jumped at his questions. "We've already ordered."

"No problem." Erik settled into the empty seat, and waved at the waiter.

He managed to keep his jaw from dropping, but Neely and Ashley weren't as subtle.

When the waiter arrived with the salads and drinks, Erik seemed to know the menu without looking. "I'll take the house salad and almond-crusted rainbow trout."

The waiter nodded, and turned to leave, but Erik stopped him. "Add a glass of Chardonnay to that." He turned and eyed their iced tea glasses. "I hope that doesn't offend you."

He had offended them, but Jon gave a one-shoulder shrug, not wanting to make an issue out of his choice of drink. The women didn't respond.

"It's nice to see you again, Neely."

"Thanks." She glanced his way, and focused on her salad.

He reached to his right, and pressed his hand against Ashley's. "And it's great to see you, too, Ashley. It's been a while, and I know you've been through some difficult times."

She gave a nod. "Yes, but I'll get through it."

He didn't move his palm pressed against her fingers. "I know you will." He finally withdrew his hand when the waiter brought his salad and drink to the table, but he didn't lay off his conversation. "I heard you have a son. What's his name?"

Her eyes brightened. "Joey. Dad asked to watch him while we came to dinner."

"Really. That was nice for you." He lifted his wineglass and held it. "Let's toast to life being the best it can be for all of us."

Ashley smiled, and lifted her glass.

Though Jon hesitated, he followed when Neely lifted hers. He observed tension in her expression, but she didn't let it control her. She clinked their glasses and returned her attention to her salad. Jon did the same, half listening to Erik's line.

Jon had barely touched his salad when the waiter brought the three entrees with the promise of bringing out Erik's shortly. With their meals on the table, Erik quieted a moment, his gaze drifting from Ashley to Neely and back.

While Jon's stomach knotted with every tick of the clock, he cut into his steak without interest. What he'd thought would be a pleasant evening had turned into a nightmare. He didn't trust Erik, and his biggest hope was that Neely meant what she said about not wanting to see Erik, let alone start a relationship with him again. Erik's unfaithfulness filled his mind, but he refused to bare that news to Neely. It smacked of gossip and jealousy. He wanted no part of it. Neely's intelligence would outshine Erik's game plan, if that's what it was.

"What made you come here today, Erik?" The question—reeking of derision and shame—trudged along his spine. He didn't treat people in that way, but Erik deserved it. He suspected somehow Erik knew they were there.

"Why do you ask?" Erik's smile faded.

"I wondered the same thing?" Neely's silence ended. "Funny you'd find us here."

"Just lucky."

Erik's answer sounded forced.

Ashley chuckled. "I don't think so. Dad mentioned a man had called asking to speak to Neely, and Dad said he hoped you didn't mind, but he told him the restaurant."

Jon's fist tightened as a smirk grew on Erik's face.

"I said I was lucky." Erik chuckled. "Lucky your dad told me where you were."

No one else laughed.

Erik grasped his wineglass, and as he did, the waiter brought his meal. Everyone quieted, concentrating on the food until Erik lay down his fork and turned to Ashley. "I'm sorry you don't have Joey with you. I'd love to meet him. Kids are a special gift. I'm sure you feel that way, too."

Jon choked on his bite of steak, and took a drink of water to wash down the beef.

Ashley gazed at Erik for a moment. "I'm surprised you

realize how special they are. That's nice. Joey is really bright, and he talks so well for his age. He's not even three."

"Really."

His exaggerated enthusiasm grated Jon as he struggled to hold back his anger.

Ashley's face lit up. "Ask Neely." She glanced at her sister.

Neely's eyes sparked, evident that she felt the same frustration.

Erik leaned closer to Ashley. "I'd love to meet him."

The sick plan emerged, and Jon had to contain the words that flew into his thoughts. Playing up to Ashley could mean only one thing. Erik was using her to get to Neely. He assumed Neely wasn't that gullible, but he could be wrong. Very wrong.

Chapter Six

Neely couldn't sleep. The memory of Erik playing up to Ashley turned her stomach. She'd tossed and turned to drift off, but even in repose, dreams assaulted her until she woke and lay staring into the dark, disgusted.

Her first plan was to warn Ashley, but then she had second thoughts. She needed to wait and see if Ashley caught on to Erik's tact. She'd told her sister her reservations about him, and hopefully Ashley would accept Neely's concerns.

She crawled out of bed to face the morning. She showered and dressed, but when she headed downstairs, her father had beaten her to the kitchen. He sat at the table, a coffee cup in his hand but no food. "Ready for breakfast, Dad?"

"An hour ago."

"I'll fix you something." She decided not to let his comment get to her. Instead of aiming for the refrigerator, she headed to the front door and collected the newspaper. Her dad had always been an avid reader, and the paper would entertain him while she prepared breakfast.

When she brought the paper to the table, he ignored it. "I should have made my own breakfast, but you keep telling me not to do anything. You know life is boring, sitting and being waited on. I'm not used to it."

She pulled out the eggs and a bowl to scramble them while she decided how to respond. Her dad was right in some ways. Life without purpose was empty. Without a job or plans for her future, even she had a hollow feeling though she'd designated her purpose as being a support for her dad and sister. Maybe they didn't need her.

She tempered her frustration. "You're right, Dad. You need to do things that aren't stressful to your heart. Breakfast is something you can do, I guess."

He grumbled as he opened the newspaper, and spread it on the table.

Her dad's behavior seemed so unlike him. He'd always been loving and kind, and since she'd arrived and started trying to help him, he'd balked at her attempts. She could walk away and leave him alone, but she'd come to help. How could she turn her back?

She dropped two slices of bread in the toaster, then beat the eggs and poured them into the frying pan. When she finished and set the plate in front of her dad, she poured a cup of coffee for herself and sat across from him. His focus remained on the newspaper as he ate, and she drew the section he'd already discarded in front of her. Though nothing in the news caught her interest, she stared at it anyway.

Her dad shoved the empty plate to the side and looked up. "Thanks. It was good."

"You're welcome, Daddy."

Daddy. Years had passed since she had called him Daddy but today she needed that connection. Her mind veered to Jonny and his relationship with his parents. He didn't talk about them much, but he'd always had good words to say about his mother and father, and she'd always felt the same. They were church people, active in their faith and raised their children to be believers, too.

Sometimes Neely wondered if that's what she lacked. She'd gone to church often with Rainie along with her parents and Jonny. Pest that he was, she admired his diligence in attending worship and participating in the youth activities. When they'd talked earlier, he'd mentioned how she'd participated in charitable events, but so had he and Rainie. Maybe that's how she'd gotten involved with helping others.

That attribute hadn't come from her parents. Though her dad had a quiet kindly attitude, one that reflected Christian beliefs, her mother attacked the poor. Why didn't they get out and find a job like everyone else? Her mom held little value for religion. How could people blindly accept that God cared one bit about them? But Neely had listened when she went to church, and she knew why Jesus had died on the cross and she'd accepted the comfort of knowing a loving God cared about her.

Ashley had gotten involved with church through Adam, and she stuck with it. That's what had given her strength during her terrible loss when he was killed. Neely still couldn't fathom how she would deal with it. Even her mother's death four years ago—and their relationship hadn't been strong—had thrown her off balance. Ashley showed a kind of strength that Neely envied.

But now she wanted to save Ashley the heartbreak of getting involved with Erik, and she needed to ask subtle questions to learn what reaction he'd had on her at dinner. His drinking might be a good turn-off for her sister.

She headed for the telephone in the living room, not wanting her father to hear the conversation. As she reached to pick up the phone, it rang.

Her chest tightened hearing Jonny's voice.

"Two questions— Would you be willing to get involved with me in some of the church's charitable activities? They're doing a number of things that I know you've always enjoyed. My second question is do you want to run tonight, or meet me at the gym when I'm off work?"

She stared at the phone, wondering which question to answer first and weighing what she really wanted to say. Part of her wanted to ease away from Jonny. He was too appealing, and she'd already considered easing him into a relationship with Ashley, although that hadn't been successful. Her pulse skipped, knowing she'd been happy that it hadn't. What was she thinking?

"What kind of charitable activities?" That was the only question that gave her time to organize her thoughts.

"The bell rang and I have to get to class. Let's talk later. How about running tonight?"

"The park?" She wanted to say no but couldn't.

"Good. I'll pick you up about three-thirty." His voice faded as if he were hanging up, but then came back strong. "Almost forgot. I have another proposition for you. See you later."

Before she could ask, he'd hung up. What kind of proposition? He'd used that phrase before. She tossed possibilities in her mind. Probably something to do with the church charitable works. But maybe not. Did it have to do with Ashley? Her chest constricted worse than before. Jonny had been amazing with Joey. The image stayed with her and made her grin. Big-shouldered Jonny and the tiny little two-year-old carrying on a conversation. Amazing.

She sank into the chair, again having second thoughts about calling Ashley. First her mind needed to be settled. What did she want for her sister? Would her sister even care about what she wanted? It was Ashley's life. Laying off her dad and sister might be what she needed to do. They survived before she returned home, and her interference only seemed to add conflict to their lives. She closed her eyes, assaulted by her questions.

When she pulled her mind free of her problems, she rose. She'd eat toast, and then set out on the errands she needed to run—groceries, her dad's prescription refills, and giving Rainie a call. She hadn't seen her since the party although they'd talked a couple times on the phone. Rainie had a good mind and often gave good advice, but her issues with Jonny were out of bounds. She longed for answers that she couldn't seem to find herself. She'd settle on one, determined to pull away from Jonny, but then the softer side of her sent her in the opposite direction. This was so unlike the girl known for her unassailable ability to follow her decisions.

"Look at the trees. The leaves are turning colors."

Jon gazed across the field to the distant trees beyond the inline track. "They're beautiful." And so was she. He watched the sunlight filter through her dark hair, striking it with reddish gold. It took him back to an autumn long ago, the one when she wore her pumpkin shirt. The vision made him grin.

"Are you going to tell me your proposition?" She gazed at him with question in her eyes.

He loved seeing her uncertain for once. Neely's confidence needed to be shaken once in a while. She'd challenged him many times in the past. The memories of those days eased through him. "Let's run first." Before he gave her a chance to rebut, he darted off, and she followed.

"Unfair."

Her voice drifted to him from behind. He slowed a little so she could catch up, flashed her a grin, and then took off again. Though he had longer legs, Neely pushed herself to the limit and wasn't too far behind him. When his lungs felt as if they would burst, he slowed to a trot, and let her catch up to him. Her cheeks were rosy from the cool breeze or maybe from exertion. He figured his looked the same. Hearing her gasping for each breath, he eased to a slow trot, and stopped. He hung his head toward the earth, and sucked in air. Neely did the same.

"You are challenging me, aren't you?" She tilted her head toward him, each of them hanging downward making the earth look cockeyed.

He tried to plant an innocent look on his face. "Would I do that?"

She rose and chuckled. "I think so. Now—" She put her hands on her hips. "While I fill my lungs, tell me your proposition."

He had two of them, and he weighed which one to suggest first. "Next Friday is homecoming, and I wondered if you'd like to go to the football game. It's home, and Rainie and Ty will be there, too. Afterward Rainie suggested we drop by the house." He studied her expression, unsure of which way she would go with her response.

"Will your parents be home?"

He let lose a chuckle. "Are you worried about chaperones?"

A grin played on her face as she gave him a poke. "No. I'd like to see them. It's been a long time."

"Yes. They'll be home as far as I know."

"Then I'll accept." Without warning, she darted off again.

He followed, glad to keep the other discussion for later, and her positive response to the homecoming bolstered his spirit. He took off, and shot past her before he slowed.

She let out a "not fair," and he slowed to run beside her. They circled the inline track three more times until he admitted it was enough. When they approached the park bench along the edge, he swung onto the seat.

Neely joined him, panting as if she'd run out of air. "Whew. That was a workout. I'm glad you're not my personal trainer." She leaned her head back a moment drawing in deep breaths.

He leaned forward, thinking of his next proposition, and wondering if he should even mention it.

She straightened her back. "I meant to tell you I did spend a day with one of the trainers, but I didn't learn much more than I already knew. So I'm good to tackle it on my own."

He patted her back and let his arm linger there a moment, enjoying the feeling of oneness. She didn't seem to resist, and that encouraged him. "I had another thing to tell you. It's the actual proposition I made reference to on the phone."

Her expression let him know he'd aroused her curiosity. "You might not be interested, but I heard yesterday they are planning to hire another clerk in the front office. I'm not sure if they want to bring someone in from the outside or transfer someone from another school in the district, but it might be a job opportunity for you if you're interested."

She remained quiet as if scrutinizing the idea. "I don't suppose they pay much." She bit the edge of her lip. "But then it's a start until I find something better, isn't it?"

"That's what I thought." He slipped his arm farther around her back and drew her to his shoulder for a moment. He didn't push his luck.

"My other option is to move back to Indianapolis. I might find some opportunities there through friends."

His stomach lurched. "You could, but I know you came here for your dad and sister, too." He hated playing the guilt card, but he did.

"You're right." She looked thoughtful. "I suppose I could drop by the school and see what it's about. Do you think that's okay? It's not a secret is it?"

He gave her shoulder a squeeze. "If it were, then I wouldn't know about it."

"I suppose so." She chuckled. Then her expression grew serious. "I've been struggling about my decision to come here, and I've been asking myself if Dad and Ashley really need my support. Coming home could have been a mistake. I seem to stir up more problems being here than being in Indianapolis."

His stomach tightened, and he scrambled to offer advice without his personal prejudice. Her sudden qualms about being home confused him. "Why do you think they don't need you?"

She shrugged, and he let his arm slip to the bench back. "Dad's upset with my trying to help him. Even my suggestion to use the bedroom down stairs riles him a little. I can't seem to do anything right."

He monitored the response that struck him as soon as he heard her reasoning. He'd learned a lot about her family, hearing Neely and Rainie talk when they were young. Neely's mother had been a controller, and maybe her dad feared she'd become one, too. But he wasn't sure he should bring it up. "Maybe your dad's been alone long enough that he thinks he can handle things on his own."

She pondered his comment for a moment. "Probably. My mom told him what to do all the time even when he'd been doing everything for her without complaint."

She'd hit the nail on the head. "Do you think your suggestions are too reminiscent of your mother's? Or maybe he misses her more than you know."

Her head lowered. "I'd never thought of that. Thanks. I really wish I knew what I could do to help without interfering."

"I can help, perhaps. If I have a chance to talk with him, I might be able to wrangle the conversation in that direction." He studied her expression for a frown but saw none. "Want me to try?"

Her expression softened. "If you're subtle. Can you be?" She arched a brow.

"Just watch me."

She chuckled, then eased upward and kissed his cheek. "Thanks. You're a nice man, Jonny."

His cheek tingled with the pressure of her kiss, and he lost himself in the moment. When he managed to gather his wits, he thanked her for the compliment but longed to remind her that a man is called Jon not Jonny. It wasn't the name. He'd been Jonny for years, but to Neely the name seemed connected to words like *pesky* and *pest* and his four-years-younger status. Calling him Jon meant he'd grown beyond those years. Would she ever let the past go?

A faint pink tinted her cheeks, and it dawned on him that the kiss surprised her as much as him.

Neely glanced at her watch, and sighed. "I should be on my way. I want to talk with Ashley."

"About your dad?"

"Dad and Erik."

The reference caught him, and he took a moment before he asked. "I know the problem with your dad. What about Erik?" He faltered, realizing his question might be too personal.

"His behavior. Didn't you think he was coming on to Ashley?"

Whew. Her comment opened the door, but he wasn't sure if he wanted to enter. No matter what he said, it could blow up in his face. "He seemed friendly."

"Too friendly. Years ago he knew Ashley, but she was my little sister and that was it. He tolerated her."

"You mean like you tolerated me?"

She blinked at the comparison. "I suppose, and now look at you. No more pesky Jonny. You're a handsome man with a good heart."

"Thanks again." Her words wrapped around him, and he wanted to tell her how much he cared about her, but he contained the desire to be that open. She knew he'd had a crush, as he'd called it, but today's feelings were far more than a boyish crush. He'd lingered in his mind all these years. But dreams were difficult because they were dreams. The dreamer didn't expect them to be real, but with Neely's return to Ferndale, his dream bordered on reality. "So what you're saying is today Ashley is a beautiful woman."

A frown flickered on her face, and then vanished. "She is." She shook her head. "What upset me were his comments about Joey. Erik never doted on kids. He went out of his way to avoid them. Do you think someone can change that much?"

He shrugged. "I didn't dote on children when I was younger."

"Sure you did. Remember the neighbor boys? I recall you keeping an eye on them in the yard, running for their ball when it rolled into the street and giving them tips on how to pitch."

His pulse skipped. "You remember that?"

"Sure." She grinned. "You remembered my dumb pumpkin T-shirt."

But he'd loved her. He turned his back on that topic. "Do you think Ashley fell for his comments?"

She raised one shoulder. "I don't know, but I want to find out—and not on the phone. I want to look into her eyes. Then I'll know."

He wished he could read Neely's eyes. Then he'd have a better grasp of what was going on in her head.

"You can talk with my dad and find out what he's thinking, but I'm the one that has to talk with Ashley."

He longed to ask her why Erik's relationship with Ashley had her concerned. Was it Erik's past or an interest in him she didn't want to admit? He didn't even hint at the question. It was safer.

Neely headed down the hallway to return to the high school parking lot after she learned job applications had to be filled out at the administration office. She should have guessed, but now she had second thoughts. When she'd stepped inside the building, she realized working at the high school bound her to memories she wasn't sure she wanted to keep fresh. Still, a job was a job. If she decided to stay in Michigan, she needed an income and medical benefits. Living at her dad's, or her sister's, wasn't an option. Though Ashley had invited her as soon as she'd heard Neely was coming home, Neely feared it would stifle both of them. Staying with her dad was temporary, but she'd lived alone too long to share a home with someone, even family.

Of course, she'd change everything if she married, but at the moment she didn't see a wedding in her future. She leaned back and drew in a breath. Why would she dismiss marriage as a possibility? Everyone wanted to be loved by that special person, and just because that special person wasn't beating on her door today, who said he wouldn't beat on it tomorrow?

Returning her focusing to the issue at hand, she learned at the office they were hiring since they were losing the woman who shifted between the attendance office and picked up the slack in the front when they were busy. The secretary invited her to speak to the principal, but it seemed senseless. The administration office took care of hiring. She wondered if it was worth giving up her workers' compensation for a salary, but the benefits were good, and the salary would depend on her qualifications.

Instead of going to her car, another idea came to mind, and she veered down the wide hallway toward the gymnasium. When she arrived, the gym was empty. A frown slipped to her face before she calculated the boys were getting ready for their next class. Disappointed, she started to step away when a door opened and Jonny came into the gym carrying some equipment. She stepped toward him.

He saw her, and a smile grew on his face. "Nice surprise."

"I decided to check out the job. I learned it has benefits, but I have to apply at the administration office."

He tossed his head back. "I should have thought of that. Sorry."

She rested her hand on his, and warmth spread through her. "Nothing to be sorry for. I appreciate your telling me about the opening."

"Mr. Turner?"

Hearing the student's voice, Neely dropped her hand.

"What, Mike?" Jonny looked past her toward the student.

She turned and saw a slender boy with acne and a shock of unruly hair.

The teen shifted from one foot to the other. "I won't be in class today. I'm sick. So I'm going home."

Jonny shook his head. "You look healthy to me."

"Really. It's my stomach."

"See you tomorrow. You don't want to miss homecoming, do you?" He flashed a grin at Neely.

"That's why I'm going home today." The boy spun around, and walked away.

Jonny shook his head again. "You never know what's up.

The kid hates PE, but if his parents gave him permission to leave, who am I to argue?" He dropped the subject, and touched her shoulder. "I've wondered about your talk with Ashley."

"We haven't talked yet. I'm heading to her place after I stop at central office. Think of me in about a half hour."

"I will." A tender look washed across his face.

The expression left her with questions. "I'll let you get ready for class." She lifted her hand in a wave.

"Neely?"

She stopped and looked back.

"I can pick you up, but you'll get here really early. Do you mind if Rainie and Ty bring you to the game, and I'll take you home?"

His forlorn look touched her. "That's fine. I'll see you tomorrow."

She returned to her car while her mind played with Jonny's expression. "Think of me in a half hour," she'd said, and his face said more than his "I will," but she didn't know what the look meant.

The stop at the administration office consisted of filling out an application and learning that someone from another building had expressed an interest in the job. That was that. They would choose someone they knew over someone they didn't, even when she'd dropped Jonny's name there, too.

Though discouraged, she bolstered herself with the knowledge that if one job appeared another would follow, and maybe one that she was better suited for. She headed for Ashley's, working on what she would say. She hadn't discussed Erik with her since their dinner with Jonny, and she hoped their conversation would be casual but enlightening.

When she pulled into the driveway, the house looked quiet, and she wondered if they were home. She walked up the steps, and reached for the bell, then hesitated. If Joey were sleeping—maybe Ashley, too—she'd awaken them. Instead she gave a couple of taps and waited. In seconds, the door opened, and Ashley grinned as she stepped back. "I was thinking of you just a few minutes ago."

Neely stepped inside, appreciating the warmth. The sun had slipped behind a cloudy sky, and she hoped if it were going to rain it would be today and not tomorrow. Bad weather would ruin the homecoming activities.

"Good to see you." Ashley kept her voice quiet as she closed the front door, and leaned against it. She looked weary.

"Joey's asleep?"

"Yes, thank goodness. I fear the terrible twos will be mild compared to the torturous threes." She chuckled. "He thinks of more things to get into. The child is too inquisitive."

"But you love him anyway." She wrapped her arm around her sister's back.

"I do. I cherish him." She motioned toward the kitchen. "Want something to drink? Eat?"

"Not now, thanks. I just left the district's administration office to put in a job application for a position at the high school."

Her sister's eyes widened. "Teaching?"

"No." She grinned, and shook her head, then explained the job possibility that Jonny had told her about.

"That's a good start." Her sister stepped away from the door. "It's not what you were doing, but it's a job. They're not easy to find."

"I know, and I don't have much hope in this one. I'm guessing they'll hire from within."

Ashley shook her head and waved her words away.

"Where's that confidence of yours?" She motioned her toward an easy chair. "Have a seat. I'm glad you came."

Neely sank into the chair while Ashley plopped on the sofa. "Jon is really nice, Neely. He reminds me a little of Adam."

The look in Ashley's eyes caused her chest to constrict. "Why's that?"

"He was so sweet with Joey. I never had the joy of watching Adam's face light up when he saw his son for the first time, but he loved kids, and I can only imagine. Jon was so good with him. I smile just thinking of how they walked side by side in conversation no less."

She attacked the emotions welling inside her. "I think Joey was doing most of the talking."

Ashley grinned. "But Jon listened. That was really sweet."

She hadn't expected the conversation to dwell on Jonny. Erik had thrown himself at her, and that's what she'd expected to hear about. She didn't know if she should be relieved or upset. Her emotions wavered from one minute to the next, and her mixed feelings about Jonny made no sense at all.

Silence hovered over them while she tried to get her thoughts in order. Mentioning Erik first was not what she planned and definitely not what she wanted.

"Is something wrong?" Ashley's grin faded.

Now what? She grasped her only possible topic. "I'm still butting heads with Dad, and that's so unnatural. Sometimes I wonder if I've made a mistake coming home."

"Pooh." Ashley waved her words away again. "You're the first person to live with him in the house since Mom died. He'd lived in silence and loneliness for all this time. Now you show up, and he doesn't know what to make of it."

Neely shrugged not sure if that made sense or not. "Do you think he misses Mom? That's what Jonny suggested."

"She was a force to be reckoned with, but he loved her just the same so I'm sure he does." She leaned back, her face contemplative. "Maybe you're too much like Mom."

"Not that again."

"It's different, though. Mom was company. He heard her puttering around the house, talking on the phone, cooking meals. Now you're doing that."

"I guess." She leaned back and closed her eyes. Maybe she'd made too much of her father's reaction to her. Ashley was right in a way.

"Speaking of dinner, Erik surprised me."

Neely's eyes flew open. "In what way?"

"He's really nice. I loved his attentiveness to Joey. He said he'd like to meet him, and I thought about that."

"And what did you come up with." The tension in her back pulsed as she waited for her sister's response.

"I would never call him, but if he called me, I'd probably let him come over. I thought he was very attentive."

"Really?"

Ashley's expression darkened. "You told me you wanted nothing to do with Erik. I didn't think you'd care."

"I don't want anything to do with him romantically." Nor do I want him to have anything to do with my sister. Her heart pounded.

"Then why the look?" Ashley leaned closer, searching Neely's face. Question sparked in her eyes.

All the reasons filtered through her thoughts, but she ignored most of them, knowing that unless she told her sister about their involvement, she would never understand. "He's a drinker, Ash. That's not the kind of man you want to get involved with."

"Who said I'd get involved? I said I'd let him drop by to meet Joey."

"Erik doesn't like kids." The words blurted from her mouth. She cringed at the expression on Ashley's face.

"People change, Neely. People mature and their values change. If I didn't know better, and maybe I don't, I'd think you still have feelings for Erik. I think you're jealous."

Heat seared her cheeks. "Jealous of you and Erik? The guy's a fake. You don't know him. Jealous. I'm so far from it. You're so wrong, Ashley. So wrong."

"I don't think so. You're too vehement about this for it to be nothing more than he drinks or—as you say—he doesn't like kids. I heard him. I think he does." She drew in a long breath as if she were reloading her gun. "Anyway you're the one who bugged me about getting out socially. You even volunteered to sit with Joey. You certainly changed your mind."

Her sister's wrath sizzled through her body, and she swallowed the words that sprang in her thoughts. Best to end the discussion now and let it go. "I'm sorry you feel that way, Ash." She glanced at her watch without purpose other than effect. "I have to go." She shot up, lifted her hand in parting and darted out the door.

When the cool air hit her, she shriveled with the image of Ashley's attack. Her ally. Her sister. How had she let this happen?

Chapter Seven

Neely snuggled deeper into her jacket, her eyes on the field as Ferndale's football team played the homecoming game on their turf. Though she tried to focus on the game, more often her interest clung to Jonny, his brown, yellow and white jacket emblazoned with an eagle emphasizing his broad back. Only once she caught Jonny gazing up at the stands. She sent him a smile and wave, but she wasn't sure he saw her.

The Eagles were ahead in the first half, but now in the last quarter, they'd dropped behind by four points when the opposing team kicked a field goal. Though she knew about touchdowns and field goals, her knowledge of the rules proved minimal, but that didn't matter. Ty answered her questions—probably dumb questions in his mind—but after the game, she wanted to let Jonny know she had watched the game and was proud of him and his team. Win or lose, the excitement of the game roused cheers and boos from the bleachers, including her.

A whistle blew and Rainie and Ty rose to their feet with a shout. She pulled her eyes from Jonny to the game. "What does the whistle mean, Ty?"

He didn't look at her, his focus glued to the field, but his answer reached her. "A penalty. Ten yards for holding."

She looked back at the game, not knowing who held whom, but apparently it wasn't good news for the Eagles. Following the huddle, the opposing team snapped the ball, and somewhere in the mass of players blocking and tackling, the Eagles had intercepted it. Cheers pierced her ears, and she joined them.

The play began again, and number thirty-nine advanced the ball to the twenty-yard line. She knew that was good because it was closer to the Eagles goal line. She eyed the clock and saw the final minute ticking away. Before she turned her eyes back to the field, screams deafened her ears, and when she looked, the Eagles had made a touchdown. The kick sailed through the goal posts, and the whistle blew to end the game. Eagles won thirty-eight to thirty-five.

Jonny ran onto the field, surrounded by his team. Number eighteen who'd made the touchdown was hoisted onto someone's back and their yell boomed into the night sky. The band played their victory song while the crowd rose and headed from the bleachers.

Ty caught her attention. "Might as well hold back. We have to wait for Jon anyway."

She nodded, watching the milling crowd hop down the bleacher seats and stairs to reach the new brick gate with the overhead metal arch announcing the Ferndale Eagles that should have glowed that night with triumph.

In the buzz of noise, she watched Jonny high-five his team members and shake hands with the fans, and she longed to be with him.

"Hey, Ty. I didn't see you earlier."

Without turning around, Neely's pulse skipped hearing

Erik's call, and in moments, without turning around, she smelled his aftershave, dampening the joy she'd felt.

"Neely, nice to see you again."

His too-close whisper caused her stomach to knot. She gave a slow turn. "I'm sure you enjoyed the game."

"I did." He faced Ty and squeezed his shoulder. "We could have sat together." He eyed the three of them. "And balanced the threesome." He gave Neely a coy grin.

She opened her mouth to tell him she was with Jonny, but that wasn't exactly the truth since it wasn't a date. She slammed her mouth shut and swallowed a rebuttal, and hoped he'd revert to his conversation with Ty, but Ty had been sidetracked by another person he knew along with Rainie, and so he stuck to her side. "It's really good to see you again. Are you doing anything tonight?"

She snatched the opportunity with relish. "Jonny and I have plans."

He studied her a moment. "That's good. I wanted to talk with you about Ashley. I really enjoyed seeing her after all these years. I hope you don't mind if I give her a call."

Her stomach flipped while bile burned in her throat. "That's your business, Erik. But I'm not sure why you'd want to. You're not a fan of children, and she's saddled with one. I think that's how you'd put it."

He rested his hand on her shoulder. "But I've changed. Can't you tell? I get a kick out of kids and look forward to having my own."

With how many women? The evil thought crossed her mind. He saw Ashley as an easy mark for his amorous interests. The picture grated on her, but she could say little. It was up to Ashley to see the truth. "Good for you, Erik. That would be an improvement."

"Hmm? Do I hear a bit of bitterness."

The comment disgusted her. "Have your hearing checked."

She turned, and walked away, joining the thinning crowd toward the exit. Not wanting Erik's presence to ruin the evening, she focused on Jonny's winning team and for homecoming, which made it special.

Her pride swelled as she reached the ground, relieved that she would be in Jonny's company and away from Erik's manipulative pandering. Why hadn't she seen it when they were dating? Apparently she'd been snowed by his line. He knew how to flatter a woman and make her feel special. He could do that with more than one at a time, she'd learned.

Relief filled her when she strode onto the field. Jonny saw her coming, and headed toward her, a smile lighted his face. She ran to him and tiptoed, planting a kiss on his lips. Her action surprised her, and she fell backward on her heels.

His gaze penetrated hers, and he drew her closer and embraced her as if he never wanted to let go. Her head spun with their unexpected interaction. Uneasy, she stepped aside as Ty arrived, and reached between to shake his hand. "Great game."

Rainie gave him a hug. "I got nervous there for a minute, but the team pulled through."

"Thanks. I'm really proud of them, and I need to head in and tell them so." He shifted his attention to Neely. "Do you want to wait, or ride to the house with Ty and Rainie?"

Her mind reeled with the option. If she stayed, they would be alone, and she didn't know what to say about the kiss. Since she'd moved back, they'd spent so many great times together the kiss seemed natural, but pressed against his chest, his response sizzled through her. She weighed his question. If she left with Rainie, she feared one of them might make reference to the kiss. She needed time to think it through. "I'll wait."

His look made her lose her breath. "Great. I won't be long." He stepped away, and then turned back. "Walk with me."

She glanced at Rainie who waved her on. "We'll see you back at the house."

She strode beside Jonny to the school and waited on a bench in the hall while he talked to the team in the locker room. She relived the surprise kiss, her mind lingering on his warm lips, soft but firm, tender but urgent. Hoping to understand her action, she tried to recall her thoughts at that moment. She had none. All she saw was Jonny's eyes drawing her in as they glowed with joy of the win. Sometimes things happened, and tonight something did.

Wrapped in thought, she jumped when Jonny appeared at her side. He extended his hand. She took it and rose from the bench. "This is a special day for me."

Jon's tender look swept over her, and from his expression, she had no idea if he referred to the team's win or the kiss. "I'm happy for you. I know everyone wants to win their homecoming game."

His brows twitched as if he found her remark perplexing. "True, but I also had something else in mind."

Heat flowed to her neck, and her cheeks burned. "I didn't mean to mislead you, Jonny. I guess the excitement of the game made me—"

Jon held up his hand. "Don't explain, Neely. Sometimes emotion is unexplainable. Try enjoying the moment, okay? I did."

Her heart tap danced against her ribs while the impetus of his words lashed her to reality. She couldn't play with Jonny's feelings. He'd admitted he'd cared for her as a boy, and as much as she wanted to let herself go, that image—the boy image—stuck in her mind like a thorn. Yet the reality she'd referred to screamed in her mind. She had enjoyed the brief kiss. Too much. "It was nice, Jonny. I think it sealed our new friendship." She barely had breath to get the words out.

He took her hand and steered her toward the exit. Once they were with his parents and his sister and Ty, the experience would be forgotten. Or would it?

Sitting in the teacher's lounge, Jon dug into the cafeteria's lunch special, mac and cheese. He took a bite, and then set his fork on the tray. He'd been confused since Friday night. Neely had kissed him. Really kissed him—and on the lips. But the outcome left him wandering a maze of confusing emotions.

He'd wanted to pull Rainie aside when they were at his parents' house after the game, but he feared that would be a mistake. Rainie hadn't kept much from Neely when they were teenagers, and he guessed she didn't keep much from her now. They were truly what his parents called bosom buddies. He couldn't trust her to tell Neely how he felt, and she would only laugh at his longtime feelings for her.

"What's up?"

Dale Nixon's voice cut through his pondering. He lifted his head, and grinned at his assistant football coach. "Just tossing around a few game plays."

"Which plays?"

Football wasn't the game he had in mind, and now he'd either have to lie or come up with a game play fast. He went for the truth. "A woman. Not football."

His friend grinned and swiveled some watery spaghetti around his fork and jabbed a piece of a meatball. "Tell me about it." He slipped the food into his mouth, and chewed.

Jon wondered why he'd gotten into it but he needed to talk with someone, and Dale seemed as good as anyone. "You're a good-looking guy, and you were single once."

"The part of about being single once is true."

Jon grinned at the guy's modesty. "What would you think if a woman kissed you? A totally surprise kiss, and you'd never kissed her before except on the cheek."

"On the cheek?" Dale nearly lost his spaghetti.

"She's a friend." The definition was weak. "To be honest, I fell in love with her years ago when she was a teen, and she's back in my life."

"That sounds promising."

"I'm not sure about that." Not at all. "But what do you think?"

"About the kiss?" A questioning look grew on his face.

"Right."

"I'd think what a kiss usually means. She's got the hots for you."

His pulse did pushups. "No. I don't think so."

"Why not?" He shook his head. "She kissed you on the lips you said. Long or short?"

He relived the moment. "Short, but not too short."

"If a woman kissed me, and it was one that I cared about all these years, I wouldn't ignore it. It means something. She's either toying with you, or she feels like you do."

"She said it sealed our friendship." He tossed the words around in his head, trying to decide if that had a hidden meaning. He didn't think so.

"Love starts with friendship. You add a little romance. The kiss. Now think of the kiss as the kick off. You snatch the ball and advance it for a first down. You gain another ten yards, then twenty. You're at the forty-yard line. Maybe the thirty. If you think time's running out, go for a field goal, or take a chance—that's what I would do—and go for the real thing. A touchdown."

The football analogy sunk in. Strategy. Move slowly. A few yards at a time. He needed a game plan, and if things didn't look good, he could always punt.

"What do you think?" Dale scraped the end of the sauce with his last meatball, and put it into his mouth.

Jon nodded. "You're right. Slow but offensive. A yard at a time. Watch for interceptions. Keep the ball in my hand." He let the game play fill his mind. Dale thought the kiss meant more than Neely claimed, and Jon hoped that he was right. "Thanks, pal."

"Anytime. A good woman is worth the wait. Slow and easy, but don't drop the ball."

Jon chuckled. "I can do that."

Dale rose and lifted his tray. "I need to get back for my next class." He grasped Jon's shoulder with his free hand. "Anytime. Anytime."

Jon leaned back in the chair, and pushed the coagulated mac and cheese around on the plate. He usually loved the stuff. He made it at home from a box. This was home cooking to him. But he'd let it get cold. He didn't want to do that to Neely. Instead of letting any more time pass, tossing around his conundrum, he would call her. Make plans for something. He'd pushed the exercise a long way. He knew it was time for something else.

Jon took a chance and pulled into Neely's driveway. He hadn't seen her since the kiss, and he didn't know how she would react now. He'd thought to call but he wanted to see her in person. He sounded like Neely when she talked about wanting to see her sister's face when they talked. Something about seeing a person's body language and facial expression helped know what their words really meant. Though he was taking a chance, he had prayed she would welcome him.

He lifted his shoulders, filling his lungs with air, and stepped from the car. At the door, he hesitated, then rang the bell and waited.

The time ticked away, and a chill ran down his back. He knew it wasn't the autumn breeze but concern. Then the knob turned.

"Jon. Good to see you." Mr. Andrews pulled back the door. "Come in."

He hesitated again before pushing himself forward. "Thanks, sir." He stood in the foyer as Neely's father closed the door, waiting for him to call to her.

"Call me Fred, Jon. You're not a boy any longer."

He nodded, glad her father noticed. Now he wished Neely would do the same.

"I suppose you came to see Neely. She's not here, but come in anyway. She should be back soon." Fred beckoned him into the living room, and he followed, sensing the man was lonely. Anyway, he'd promised Neely he'd talk to her dad.

Jon sank into the chair across from her dad's recliner, but his mind was blank.

"I think Neely's checking on a job or something." He slipped into the recliner. "She has an interview, I think."

His neck snapped up. "At the school?"

"Something like that." He lifted the footrest, stretched his legs in front of him and folded his hands across his belly. "I guess a job means she's planning to stay in Ferndale awhile."

Jon shuffled words around in his head not sure what he should tell him. "I think that's her plan." Finally an idea sparked. "You enjoy having her back home, I suppose." He studied Fred's expression.

"Yes." Fred tilted his head upward as if contemplating his response. "Most of the time."

A chuckle rose in Jon's throat, too late to control. "Families have their moments."

Fred's eyes glinted as his mouth eased to a subtle grin.

"I worry she'll become her mother one day, and I try to ward that off. Know what I mean?"

He understood, but he didn't want to admit it.

"Marion was a good woman, but it was her way or no way. I do things—even things I know aren't best for me so Neely doesn't think she's in charge." He shook his head. "But that girl is determined."

This time Jon laughed. "She is. I've known her long enough to recognize that attribute."

Her father slapped his leg. "I keep her on her toes, and it gives me a kick." He dropped the footrest and leaned closer as if he feared she had sneaked in the back door and would hear him. "I watch her squirm, but then I feel bad, too. You know."

Jon had to agree with that. He had a difficult time putting anyone he cared about in a difficult position, but sometimes it seemed necessary to make them see the truth. He might have to go that route with Neely.

Her father ran his fingers through his thinning gray-tinged hair. "But I love that girl." He looked away a moment again as if in thought. "I don't want her to stay here for me. That's the real problem. She had a good job in Indianapolis. Now she's here where good jobs are hard to find."

Jon watched Fred's eyes search his as if for an answer. He didn't have one, but now he knew the real problem that caused the tension between them. Though what could he do with it? If he told Neely, he would ruin the confidence her father had in him and probably cause more problems than solutions.

Her dad flipped the footrest up. "I can't control her life, either. If she finds work and is happy here, then I'll assume that's what's meant to be."

"That's a good philosophy, sir...Fred. I think that's all you can do." He wrapped the words in his heart, assuming what happened was meant to be. God was in control. Not him or not Neely or not her father. He had to trust in the Lord.

A rattle from the foyer jerked their attention. Both turned toward the doorway as Neely stepped into the opening.

"Hi." Her gaze drifted from his to her father's and back. "This is a surprise."

"It was for me, too." He tried not to flinch—not even blink—but keep his eyes aimed at hers. She turned away first, and looked at her dad. "You and Jonny are having a good visit?"

He chuckled. "Waiting for you, yes. You don't think this young man came to visit with me, do you?"

Jon flinched this time, although he'd spoken the truth, but it emphasized the man's loneliness, and he wished he could help. "Do you like to walk, Fred?"

Neely's chin drew back when she heard him call her father by his first name.

"Used to go for walks. Haven't been, and now I have the warden keeping her eyes on me." He turned away from her and gave Jon a subtle wink.

"Dad, that's not nice. I'm not a warden. I'm…" She tossed up her hands. "Never mind." She pivoted, and marched down the hall.

Jon wanted to follow her, but it was their battle. All he could do was try to give her discerning guidance dealing with her father.

Fred scratched his head. "You see. She can't even take a joke."

"I think she missed the wink."

Fred chuckled, then hoisted himself from the chair, and went to the doorway. "How did your interview go?" He waited and, not hearing a response, he shrugged. He lumbered back to the chair. "I probably should walk. I'll be a doddering old man soon, older than my sixty-eight years."

"I'll stop by when I can. We can walk together if you'd like."

Fred eyed him for a second. "I'm sure you have an ulterior motive but that's a nice offer. I'll take you up on it sometime."

"Great, and I'm sure Neely would enjoying walking with you, too. She's trying to get exercise."

"Who wants to get exercise?" Neely stood in the doorway. She'd taken off her skirt and jacket and wore jeans and a sweatshirt.

Jon admired her no matter what she wore. "Your dad was talking about walking, and I said you'd probably enjoy walking with him since you're—"

"Trying to get exercise." She grinned. "I figured that out." She wandered into the room, and plopped on the sofa. "And I need to exercise since I'll be sitting a lot with the new job."

Jon bolted forward. "You got it."

She nodded. "Daddy, you'll be happy to get rid of me for a whole day won't you?"

He shook his head. "Not really. Too quiet. No one to fight with."

She flickered a grin as she crossed the room to kiss his cheek. "I'll be at the high school in the front office."

Her dad slapped his leg. "Now she'll be telling *you* what to do, Jon."

He grinned at Neely, hoping to waylay tension between them. When he saw her face, he realized his reaction wasn't necessary. Neely must have thought about what had happened when she changed clothing. At this moment, she was in good spirits.

"You two should go out and celebrate the job."

Jon turned and eyed Neely's father. He saw a new sparkle in his eyes, and matchmaking was in the glint. He wanted to give the man a hug, but obviously that wasn't appropriate. He searched Neely's face, but she hadn't caught on or else covered up her reaction well. "What do you say?"

She turned her head his way. "Would you like to go, too, Daddy?"

"Naw." Fred waved her questions away. "I'm looking forward to yesterday's leftovers. I loved the casserole. It was like your mother used to make."

Neely shifted her focus from her father to him. "Are you sure?"

This time he smiled. "Never surer. Ferndale High has just hired a supreme clerk for the front office."

"Clerk?" She put her hand on her hip. "I'm taking over the attendance records. They thought I had better organizational abilities than the woman vying for the job from the middle school."

"I'm glad they recognized your abilities." Jon's heart clinched, recognizing her kissing abilities as supreme. "That is something to celebrate." He stuck out his hand, and she slipped hers in as he guided her toward the front door. He wanted to call out a hooray to Fred, but he controlled himself. He was thrilled he had at least one person on his side.

Chapter Eight

Neely rang Ashley's bell, waited with no response, and then opened the door. "It's me, Ash."

A sound came from somewhere in the house, and she stepped inside. The living room was empty and the kitchen, but the noise sounded closer. She walked to the basement stairs and listened. The slosh of water and the clank of a metal door answered her question. "Ash, I'm here."

In a moment, her sister appeared at the bottom of the steps, wearing no makeup and her hair disheveled. She gave a wave and held up her index finger. "I'll be up in a minute."

Neely strode to a cabinet and withdrew a glass. She turned on the tap, filled the tumbler with cold water, and then leaned against the counter and took a lengthy drink. What she wanted to talk about with Ashley was the day she kissed Jon. She wanted to know why she'd done it since she'd been determined not to get involved with her old nemesis. But the more she thought the more she realized she was the nemesis, not Jonny. He'd been kind all the time when she gave him a chance. She'd been the one who'd made snide comments and belittled him.

But the desire to talk about it faded. The kiss would

remain her secret. Hers and Jonny's. Admitting it would just arouse speculation with Ashley, and Neely didn't need anyone matchmaking or pushing her to give Jonny a chance. This was something she needed to handle without anyone confusing the issue.

Every time she thought of that day, she winced at the strong urge she'd experienced to kiss him, and then it happened. She'd cut the kiss short, but that had been her willpower and not desire. His lips were warm and soft, giving but not demanding. She'd melted to a puddle in that moment, and only her strong will made her draw back. Then reality set in of what she'd done.

She'd never forget the look on Jonny's face. It had been unreadable, because so many emotions seemed to filter in his eyes. Sometimes she wondered if his crush, as he called it, had remained this whole time. But then she scoffed at the idea. What man would continue to have feelings for a woman who'd vanished from his life for years and had been a pain to him when she was around?

When the basement door closed, she faced Ashley. "Hope I'm not interrupting your laundry day."

Her sister chuckled. "When you have a two-year-old, every day is laundry day." She motioned toward the table. "Have a seat." Her gaze drifted to her glass. "I have pop. Would you—"

She lifted the tumbler. "Water is fine. I dropped by on a whim. I've been wanting to talk to you since our little tiff a while back. It's been on my mind, and on homecoming, we couldn't discuss it and I need to apolog—"

"Forget it." Ashley's palm flashed upward. "Neither of us is perfect. We both make mistakes. I'm sorry, too."

Neely stepped forward and gave her sister a hug. "I also want to tell you about my job. I start Monday."

Ashley's head drew back. "You got it? At the high school?" She filled a tumbler with cola.

Her head bobbed yes as she told her sister about the job offer and what she would do at the high school. "It's not what I would have looked for, but it's convenient for now, and I think I can use a break from the corporate world. Everything is so unstable."

"Wise, and who knows if you want to stay here. You may get the urge to go back to your friends in Indiana."

The idea knotted in her chest. That had crossed her mind, but too many reasons incited her to stay in Michigan. "Right now that's not a plan. I want to keep my eye on Dad, although I've bungled at that."

Ashley turned from the counter, holding a tumbler. "That's still a problem?" She turned away and opened the refrigerator.

"When I talked with Jonny, he told me that Dad should exercise. I've been trying to stop him from doing much of anything. In fact, Jonny offered to take walks with Dad. I could do that, but I worried about him getting too tired, and—"

"You're worried because he's our dad. Think logically. Exercise is good for everyone in the proper doses."

Releasing a sigh, Neely nodded. "I realize that now. I didn't believe a thing Jonny told me, so I looked up heart attack care on the internet, and he was right."

"He's a PE teacher." She rolled her eyes. "Obviously the guy knows about exercise and what's good and what isn't. Why don't you trust him? He's not an imbecile as you seemed to think."

Guilt rocked her. "I never thought he was an imbecile. Just a pest."

"Get over it." She shook her head. "I think he's a great

guy. Any woman would be blessed to have him as a friend. Even a husband."

"I know." The truth swept through her.

"And now you'll be working in the same building with him. You'll have to show respect. He's a teacher and a coach. He's admired by all the sport fans in the area, I'm sure. He's led the Eagles to victory many times, and the basketball team won a big trophy last year for something. I don't know a thing about basketball."

"Neither do I." And she should if she planned to be Jonny's friend.

Ashley took a sip of her drink as a distant look grew in her eyes. "I'd better check on Joey. He's sleeping longer than usual." She rose, and strode through the doorway.

Certain from her distracted look that Joey wasn't the only thing on Ashley's mind, she pondered what it might be. Memories of Adam, maybe? Comparing her again to their mother? Whatever, Ashley had something on her mind.

She slipped through the doorway. "He's fine. I'll let him sleep. He did get up extra early today. My morning quiet didn't quite happen." Ashley grinned, and settled back into the chair.

"What's on your mind?"

A frown grew on her face. "What do you mean?"

"You were distracted for a moment. I know you, Ash. Something's bothering you."

She saw her sister's face flicker, and knew she'd been right.

"Fine. I don't want to start another argument so I hesitate to tell you." She lowered her eyes and studied the moisture on the outside of her glass.

"Tell me what?" But she already knew.

"Erik called me, and he's coming over to meet Joey tonight."

Neely tried to camouflage her utter disgust. "Maybe he's changed. I could be wrong." But she knew she wasn't.

Her eyes widening announced Ashley's surprise. "Thanks for admitting that. I don't want Erik's attention to me to cause troubles between us."

"Me, neither." She studied her sister's glowing face as she looked forward to Erik's visit, but she couldn't believe what he said anymore, and she wondered if he were using Ashley in the attempt to make her jealous. Erik would do most anything to get what he wanted. From his actions, he obviously wanted her back in his life.

Jon sidled a look at Fred as they headed around the periphery of the park. Though the weather was cool, the energy they'd burned as they walked made it perfect. He hadn't said anything about Neely to her father. He didn't want to arouse his curiosity about what kind of interest he had in the man's daughter. At this point, Jon wasn't sure, either—unless he listened to his heart.

"Did I tell you my daughter had a rebirth?"

Confused, Jon eyed Fred. "No. What happened?"

"She must have listened to you—she doesn't listen to anyone usually—and she went to her computer to check things out. Probably to prove you wrong. It didn't work. She came to me with a hangdog expression, and told me what she'd read."

Jon grinned at her father's joy in seeing her eat crow. "She really admitted I was right."

He gave him an arched brow. "I wouldn't go that far, but she told me what she'd read, and guess what."

"What?"

"She said going up the stairs was good for me so I was

smart to keep my bedroom upstairs." He chuckled. "I thought it was a good idea, too, since I didn't plan to use the guest room on the first floor. Marion and I shared our room for years. It's still home to me. I hadn't planned to budge."

Hearing reference to Fred's wife always gave him a start. He knew from Neely that her mother held an iron fist over her father, but from what he'd just heard, he loved her just the same. "Stairs are good for you and so is walking."

"She admitted that, too." He pulled out a hanky and blew his nose.

Jon wasn't sure if it was emotion or the fresh air.

"That girl is quite a woman, don't you think?"

Jon flinched, then realized Fred has his eyes glued to his expression. What could he say? "No denying it. You have an amazing daughter."

"Too bad some good man doesn't snatch her up. Ever think of marrying, Jon?"

His heart dipped to his toes, and shot back up to his throat. He swallowed to keep from choking. "One day I will."

"Then it has crossed your mind."

Jon couldn't help but chuckle. "The idea's made a few trips across my cranium, but it never stopped. It just kept going."

Fred gave him a coy look. "One day the idea will get lodged in your chest. Then you're a goner."

"You're probably right." He managed to keep his voice steady. "Let's pick up the pace a little." Hopefully Fred's air would be used for breathing and not talking.

He did stay silent, and they made their way around the park and then headed down the sidewalk toward his house. As they approached, he saw Neely's car in the driveway. His pulse sparked, and took away the little breath he had.

"You coming in? You'd probably like something to drink, right?"

He analyzed the expression on Fred's face and knew what he wanted him to do. "Sure. But just for a couple of minutes."

Fred grinned and opened the front door. When they stepped inside, Jon heard Neely, and from the sound of the oven door closing, he knew she'd been working in the kitchen. Before he could get there, she'd stepped into the dining room and spotted him. "Jon." She motioned behind him. "I see you and Dad went for a walk."

"And a good one, too. Nice and brisk." Fred gave him a wink.

Neely eyed Jon, and he hoped she saw from his face to let it drop.

A faint grin slid to her mouth. "Glad you had some good exercise."

He grunted as if disappointed that she hadn't taken the bait. "I'm heading upstairs for a few minutes. You two go ahead and talk. I'm sure you can manage that." He started up the stairs as his chuckle greeted them.

"Your dad's quite a character." He wondered what she would say if she knew about her father's matchmaking attempts. Not even subtle. He'd been blatant. But Jon didn't mind. He liked having someone significant on his side.

She nodded but no smile. "I'm glad you came."

That comment wasn't what he'd expected. He tilted his head, waiting for her to tell him why.

"Dad probably told you I decided to get off his back about the downstairs bedroom."

She arched a brow.

Jon couldn't stop his smile. "Yes, but here's something you might not know." As he spoke, he wondered if that's something he shouldn't mention, but it was too late. "I think being in that room reminds him of your mom. That might have been a place he felt close to her."

Her face flickered with surprise. "I've never thought of that. I suppose it was one place that she showed her softer side." She looked away and then returned her gaze. "That's nice to know."

"I thought it might be meaningful. He loved her despite her controlling nature."

"He did. Ashley said the same thing to me." She lowered her head as if in thought. "Maybe realizing that will help me get over some of the frustration I've hung on to even after Mom's death."

He drew closer and touched her shoulder. "We may learn lessons late, but learning the lesson is the important thing. You've done that."

She nodded and tilted her chin. "Thanks." She gazed away a moment. "I've learned something else today."

His pulse revved. "What?"

She blew out a stream of air. "It's what I expected…we expected. Erik called Ashley, and he's seeing her tonight. Reason? He wants to meet Joey." She closed her eyes and shook her head. "In a pig's eye."

"Why not? Meeting Joey is way to get to know Ashley."

Her head bobbed upward, sadness on her face. "If I thought that were the truth. If I thought he had changed. I'd be all for it. He has money and prestige. He could give her a good life, but I think he has another motive."

He could guess, but he wanted to hear it from her. "What's the other reason?"

"To make me jealous. Erik doesn't like to lose something he thinks he should have. I'm guessing it's me."

His chest tightened, but he asked anyway. "Would that be possible?"

"Never. Even if he's made a hundred-and-eighty-degree

turn, and I doubt if that would happen. He's divorced and that happened for a reason. I'd love to know what that reason was."

Jon kept his mouth closed. Though her answer to his question gave him assurance, he couldn't be positive. Her preoccupation with Erik bothered him. He didn't know why but it did.

"Maybe that's something you can let go in time, Neely. Pray that Ashley doesn't get hurt in the situation. Erik's motive is his problem, but your sister's well-being is what we'll pray for."

She reached up and pressed her hand to his, still resting on her shoulder. "I will pray for her, Jonny. You're right."

She lifted her gaze and his focus drifted to her lips. His heart tripped and his knees nearly gave way. The longing threw him. She looked more fragile than he'd ever seen her, and he sensed her concern was real. Erik had hurt her, but according to her, she'd been the one to break off the relationship. He'd thought about it, but it never made sense.

Her eyes met his, and his hand drifted down her arm and slipped around her back. He drew her closer, and she leaned her head against his chest. He feared she might hear the thrumming of his heart like a long-forgotten love song.

As she tilted her head upward, his gaze slipped to her lips, slightly parted, almost in waiting. He grasped for courage, then he lowered his mouth to hers.

"What's for dinner?"

Jon yanked away from her lips nearly giving himself a whiplash. Neely slipped from his grasp as her father entered the kitchen.

"Baked pork chops, Daddy. I'll make a salad, and we can put potatoes in the microwave." She began to bustle as domestic duties took over, but Jon knew the real reason.

"Remember, the internet said you need to eat healthy. Five fruits and vegetables a day."

The color on Neely's cheeks told him she was ruffled by her father's sudden appearance. He would have laughed at her reaction if her father's "what's for dinner" hadn't stopped him cold from kissing her the way he'd been wanting to for weeks.

He shifted toward the door, knowing the situation was going nowhere but down. "I need to get going." He lifted his hand in a wave. "Thanks for the walk, Fred, and see you again sometime, Neely."

He scooted through the doorway before he had to respond to another comment or question. His disappointment consumed him. In his mind, he'd tasted her lips and felt their soft touch. Imagination wasn't enough anymore. He wanted the real thing, and if he couldn't make it work, then he needed to get out from under her spell.

But how? He'd tried for years.

Chapter Nine

Neely stared at the computer screen in the attendance area of the office, her mind sailing between the multiple attendance forms she'd had to fill out for sick kids and a variety of other excuses to the near kiss that left her reeling. If her father hadn't broken the trance, the kiss would have happened, and she would have melted into it. She knew that as sure as she knew her name.

The common-sense side of her thanked her father for breaking the spell. Her emotional side hadn't wanted it to end. With her brain and heart in constant battle, she wavered between tossing caution to the wind or barricading herself against the unexpected longing she'd felt since getting to know Jonny again. If he were only the boy she once knew, her distance would be easy. Jonny the man—Jon—she couldn't fight his charm. She needed to cling to the Jonny she'd known.

"How's your first day?"

Her hand jerked against the keys, and the letter *K* scooted across the page. When she looked at him, she hoped her thoughts weren't engraved on her expression. "Okay, I think." She focused on the monitor and used the backspace key to delete the row and a half of *K*s.

"Sorry." Jonny chuckled, gazing at her deletion. "I guess I scared you."

"I was engrossed." But not in her typing. She'd been engrossed in him. In her feelings. In the kiss that still hung in her memory. "What's up?"

"It's my prep hour. No practice tonight so I wondered if you'd like to get together?"

Her pulse skipped. "I don't think so tonight." She searched her mind for a plausible reason. She wanted to know what was happening between Ashley and Erik, but then she didn't want to know. Another wavering situation but this one none of her business. When she looked up, Jonny had an expectant expression on his face, obviously wanting to know why. She didn't know.

"Anything wrong? How's your dad?"

"He's fine. I've been trying to feed him well. He'd live on fast food if I let him."

He nodded, but the look hadn't gone.

Stymied, she segued to a new topic. "If you want to walk with Dad tonight that would be fine."

He stared at her monitor, now clear of her extended Ks. "That's not quite what I had in mind."

She bit her lip, wishing she could release the qualms she clung to. Being with him in a crowd wasn't the problem. Alone meant danger. Digging she found her answer. "Did you want to come for dinner? Dad enjoys talking with you."

Jonny studied her a moment. "Thanks but no. Another time." He turned and strode from the office without looking back.

A hollow feeling washed over her as if she'd ignored her heart.

"Jon. I haven't seen you for a while."

Cindy batted her eyes from behind the counter, and Jon's

skin crawled. "I've been around, but with the school sports, I don't always find time for myself." Only when it came to Neely, but he couldn't say that to Cindy. She'd come on to him often, and he'd tried to ignore it, but once in a while, he wondered if Cindy would be what he needed to make Neely jealous. Maybe. He needed something that would check whatever held her back.

"I saw your last game. It was great, Jon. I'm sure you're proud of the team." She leaned on the counter, aiming for a provocative pose but he kept his gaze glued to her face.

"Thanks." He lifted his hand and scooted past as quickly as he could. The temptation to invite her out for a coffee had entered his mind, but he'd never used anyone for his purpose and never to get a date with someone else.

He strode into the locker room, and stepped into his gym clothes, stored his possessions in a locker and headed toward a weight machine. He adjusted the weights and the pulley, then sat on the incline bench to work out his upper-chest muscles. Placing his hands on the bars, he kept his elbows in line with his hands and pulled. When the burn increased, he switched his grip to target his triceps.

His concentration on Neely helped the time fly yet added tension to his workout. He had to do something to make her aware of his feelings and his determination. Neely wasn't the only one who could persevere when the motivation was right.

The conclusion that returned to him dealt with charities. Neely's attitude mellowed when she helped others, and that was the idea he'd finally struck upon. His church had announced that Welcome Inn, a day shelter for the homeless, needed churches to help prepare meals. Neely cooked with confidence, and she loved to help charities. The situation opened a door for him, and now all he needed to do was introduce the opportunity.

His arms and chest ready for a break, Jon rose and headed for the leg press. He settled onto the leg extension machine, adjusted the seat and put his feet low on the plate, and then began the donkey-kick motion. He buried his thoughts into the powerful movement, and when he drew his mind away from the hard work, his stomach flipped. Neely had entered the gym, and was heading across the room toward the stair climber. She hadn't mentioned exercising as she often did and her appearance surprised him. She'd worn exercise shorts and a knit sleeveless top that showed the soft curve of her arm.

His blood pumped like a geyser, and he looked away to control his emotions. No matter how he longed to get her out of his system, she remained. He drew in a breath, wishing away the constant memories of her, but his wishes failed. She'd returned to Ferndale, and he believed that God had a purpose for every event in the lives of His children, good or bad. As yet, Jon had no idea how his feelings for Neely would fall, but he had to trust and have faith.

With his plan B sketched out, he let trust be his guide as he put his plan into action. Since Neely hadn't noticed him, he continued to work out, not wanting to look too eager. Maybe she'd notice him first. He avoided a direct gaze, but an occasional subtle look provided him with her whereabouts, and when she moved to the treadmill, he shifted to the elliptical machine since it was closer to her. She still didn't see him or if she had, she'd managed to fool him.

When she climbed off and draped a towel around her neck, Jon did the same, stirred by her trim body, one that she'd honed since her arrival.

When her gaze shifted to him, a look of surprise heightened her skin tone. "Jonny." She took a step closer.

"You didn't mention exercising." Her expression etched with curiosity.

"Neither did you." He flashed a quick smile and didn't move.

She pulled the towel from her neck, dragged it across her face and stepped closer.

His pulse revved as he organized plan B. When she stopped beside him, he grasped the opportunity. "I forgot to tell you my church is beginning its winter schedule for one of our charities."

She twirled the towel around her hand. "What's the charity?"

"Welcome Inn. It provides day care and other services to the homeless. They're served breakfast, and we prepare hot lunches and freeze them so they always have meals ready to serve in the afternoon."

Interest flashed on her face.

He waited, but she didn't respond.

"I know you like to cook, so if you're interested, we'll be starting in two weeks."

She bit the corner of her lip, her eyes shifting from him to her towel.

He could almost hear the gears cranking in her head. He'd intentionally left it open ended. Now she could assume he hadn't presented the invitation for her company but for her contribution to the charity. He had both in mind.

"If you're interested, let me know." He turned and motioned toward the registration desk. "Cindy wants to see me so I'd better go."

A frown flickered across her brow, and her gaze shot upward toward the doorway.

"See you at school." He gave a casual wave, and strutted toward the locker room. When he'd vanished from her sight, he released a breath and asked himself why he'd brought

up Cindy. He'd already decided that he didn't use people, and now he'd done it. To make it right, he needed to talk with Cindy just to be nice, and he feared that could get him into trouble.

Neely walked in the door from another workday at the school. Though the job was fine, she realized it wasn't what she wanted to do forever. Not knowing where her life was headed had become a struggle. The experience of being home with family and loving it lay on her heart in a new way. She wished she could have enjoyed time with her mother, but she'd harbored resentment for the way her mother had treated her dad and most of the family. Now she'd begun to realize her mother's unhappiness reflected in her critical manner.

Being unfulfilled could tangle a person's secure life into resentment and create a love-hate relationship with life and those in it. She could see herself getting caught in that web. Her feelings about Jon snagged her every way she turned. It had become a contest between her determination to resist him or her option to take a chance and live with the results. The idea was a new one that scared her.

And another situation, she'd talked for a short time with Ashley and learned that her evening with Erik had been wonderful, except he'd arrived too late to meet Joey. He'd already fallen asleep and her sister had put him in bed. Why didn't that surprise her? Whatever Erik's excuse, Ashley had accepted it with no question. Neely closed her eyes. Was this another example of her critical nature?

Letting the question fade, she dropped her handbag in a chair and listened for her father. She heard nothing. The kitchen was empty, and the only other option was his room. She strode to the staircase. "Dad." She waited. She bounded up the steps and halted halfway. "Dad?"

A pain shot through her chest as her blood constricted. "No." She darted to the top and shot to his closed bedroom door. "Dad?" Nothing. She burst inside and faltered. He wasn't there. She looked around. The blankets had been pulled up and the pillow tossed on top. She rounded the bed, fearing what she'd find on the other side. Only his slippers sat together on the rug.

She darted to the hallway but noticed the bathroom door was open. Air shot from her lungs as she scurried down the stairs and opened the hall closet. His lightweight jacket was missing. She dragged air through her lungs, shaking her head at her foolish fear. He'd gone for a walk or maybe... No. She spotted his car keys on the table near the foyer doorway. Walking. That was the answer.

She sank into a chair and covered her face, sorting through the emotions she'd experienced. Love had power she didn't understand, emotions she'd never experienced before. She straightened and leaned against the cushion while memories of what she'd thought was love flooded through her. Though her heart would patter when she first met Erik, she'd been more flattered by his attention than wrapped in love. She realized that now for the first time.

Ashley had questioned her about love, and she'd never known it the way her sister described it. *Part of me feels empty as if something is missing. I want to feel whole again, but it will take someone special.* The only time she'd felt empty was the last time she'd seen Jonny. She'd felt hollow as if her heart had been... The realization washed over her like a flood. She lost her breath in the memory. What was she doing with her life?

The sound of the back door opening stirred her to rise and get a grip. Lately her dad seemed to study her as if he were looking into her mind through her eyes. She wanted no one to look in her head since she had no idea what they would see. When she swung through the kitchen doorway, she stopped cold.

Jonny stood behind her father, a fleeting smile lighting his face. "Hi."

She gave a nod to Jonny, confusion railing her senses. "Dad, I was worried about you."

"It's my fault." Jonny stepped around him and braced his hand on a kitchen chair. "I called him from school and asked if he'd like to walk. I guess we didn't think to tell you."

"Tell her?" Her dad gave a chuckle. "She's not my keeper. Are you, Neely?"

She pondered the comment. "I guess I'm not." That had been her mother. His keeper with a whip. "I didn't expect you to be out, but exercise is good." She turned to Jonny, fearing to look in his eyes. "Thanks. That was thoughtful."

He shrugged. "I wanted to get out anyway. This time of year is fleeting. Once the snow falls that puts a damper on walking."

Finally she looked into his eyes, her chest constricting. "Have a seat." She motioned to the chair his hand rested on. "How about a pop? Cola? What's your choice?"

Her dad lapped his jacket over his arm. "Give the man a cup of coffee. It's getting nippy out there."

She strode to the coffeemaker as Jonny slipped off his jacket, hung it on the chair back and sat. Seeing him now sent her thoughts back to the last time they'd spoken. He'd said he'd see her at work but he hadn't. Sometimes he'd pop into the office just to say hi and see how she was doing, and occasionally they ran into each other in the lunch room, but that hadn't happened, either. Was he avoiding her? The question entered her mind more than once.

And then there was Cindy. She'd watched the woman flirt with him at the fitness center. He'd seemed to be polite but didn't fall for her come-ons. But the last time they'd spoken, he'd mentioned Cindy wanted to see him. If something was going on, she wanted to know before she made a fool of herself...if she hadn't done that already.

She'd filled the coffeemaker in a trance, and when enough had dripped into the pot to fill a cup. She opened the cabinet, pulled one down and filled it. When she turned, Jonny's eyes were on her. She set the cup in front of him, and then returned to find the low-calorie chocolate chip cookies she'd baked for her dad—amazing what almond flour and sugar substitute could do.

Though he had left the kitchen, at the scent of the coffee, her dad returned. She poured him a cup but he only grabbed a couple of the cookies and left again, leaving her to face Jonny alone. She grasped a cookie and slipped into a chair across from him. "I appreciate your spending time with my dad. I know he enjoys company."

"He's a good man, and he's filled with wisdom."

A frown tugged at her forehead. "What kind of wisdom?" Her dad offering wisdom was unexpected. Yet her attitude had been tainted by her mother's influence.

"Your dad has a grasp on life and faith that's worth hearing."

"He is a man of faith. I saw that with the love he continued to shower on my mom even when it wasn't returned."

His jaw tightened when he looked at her. "Wouldn't it be great if we could all be that way?"

The comment threw her. Beneath the words, she sensed a meaning that she didn't comprehend. Was he referring to her feelings for Erik? If so, he didn't realize that neither of them knew anything about love back then. They still didn't as far as she could see. Though she longed to ask

Jonny to explain, she closed her mouth to give his comment more thought.

"I'm learning new things about Dad every day. My time here has been good, I think. It's opened up windows with a fresh perspective on life in general, but most about me as part of it."

His eyes searched hers. "I'm glad, Neely. I want you to be happy. I think you deserve it."

"No more than anyone else." She studied him, longing to know what was going on in his head. She'd never know if she didn't listen and open her mind.

Her memory shot back to the last time they'd talked. "Tell me more about your church's work with charities." She rose and poured herself a cup of coffee, then brought the pot back to refill his.

"Right now, we'll be focused on Welcome Inn and help for Haven, a home for abused women and their children. Then we'll have a food collection around Thanksgiving for the homeless and our own food bank. The Giving trees happen at Christmas. They put up ornaments with people's names and gift suggestions. These are given to various organizations." He lifted his cup and took a sip. "You used to help Rainie with some of those things years ago."

His face had brightened, and the memories warmed her, too. "You, Rainie and me." She lifted her gaze to his. "I'm surprised how much time I spent with you back then."

He drew in a ragged breath that surprised her. "Those were good days."

"Actually they were." She reached across the table and pressed her hand against his. "I'm sorry that I didn't appreciate you then, Jonny."

"You mean you do now?"

He placed his other hand over hers, cocooning hers in his warmth. The heat rolled through her. "I do."

"We'd better eat. Ashley will be here soon."

Her dad's voice jolted them, and they pulled apart their hands. "Ashley? What's up?"

"I'm taking care of Joey." Her dad looked away. "While she goes out with Erik." He ambled deeper into the room. "You'd think I had my fill of that guy years ago, but here he is again after another one of my daughters."

Jonny's eyes bore through her.

She struggled to control her reaction, but she knew she'd failed. "A stroke of bad luck, Dad." She tried to keep her voice light as she headed for the refrigerator. "How about the rest of that spaghetti, I made?" She turned to her dad. "We have plenty, Jonny."

"No. I'd better get home." He pushed back his chair, rose and carried his cup to the sink. "I'll see you later."

When? That's what she wanted to know. Whenever Erik was mentioned, he seemed to withdraw. "If you're sure. I really have plenty."

"I'm sure." He slipped on his coat and headed toward the back door. "I'll go out this way."

"Jonny?" She stepped toward him, but she forced herself to stop.

"I'm sure you'll want to talk with Ashley." He opened the door. "Alone."

Before she could respond, he closed it. She moaned. If she let her past control her future she would remain stagnant. She returned to the refrigerator, deep in thought.

Chapter Ten

Two days passed and Jonny still hadn't stopped by the attendance office. Neely struggled with what to do. She understood his aversion to Erik. Allowing Erik's presence to control her life had been a mistake and one that accomplished nothing but creating more bad memories. Now the bad feelings had spread to Jonny, she feared.

To her surprise, she'd controlled her comments to Ashley. She'd said nothing about the date and waited for Ashley to report how it went. But Ashley had kept quiet too.

Progress required action. She knew Jonny's schedule and had resolved to do something to get their relationship back on track. Losing his friendship hurt, and she blamed herself. When his prep hour arrived, she headed to the gym, but didn't see him there. Hoping he wasn't in the men's locker room or someplace she couldn't enter, she took the hallway to the teachers' lounge. When she opened the door, she saw him, his nose buried in a sports magazine.

She stepped inside and stood a moment, waiting for him to notice her. He didn't so she took the initiative. "Good article?" She sank into the chair near him.

He looked up as if surprised. "It is." He turned the magazine over and lay it on the table. "Problem?"

"No. I just…" Her lungs locked. "I miss you."

His brow arched before he spoke. "You do?"

She nodded, unable to get her tongue wrapped around the words lodged in her throat. What could she say that didn't unveil more than she wanted to admit? "It's still fairly nice weather. Do you want to run tonight?"

He tapped the table with his thumb a moment. "I can't."

She mumbled an "oh." But then she took a brave step. "You have plans with Cindy?"

"Cindy?" He shook his head. "No. Where would you get that idea?"

Heat charged to her cheeks, and she lifted her eyes to heaven asking herself why she'd mentioned Cindy.

"I called your dad a while ago and we're walking… unless you want to join us."

Drowning in mortification, she shook her head. "I'll let you two walk. Maybe another time."

He studied her a moment. "Join us, Neely. We can't really run but—"

"It's good for Dad to have your company without me butting in." She shrugged. "Man to man." She lowered her eyes to garner courage. "I'm sorry I brought up Cindy. You'd mentioned talking with her the other day and I assumed—"

He shook his head. "Nothing's going on between us. Not that she wouldn't like that." He grinned.

"I noticed." Heat continued to burn her cheeks.

"You did?" He arched his brow again.

She nodded. When he didn't say anything else, she slid the chair back and rose. "I'd better get back to work."

He appeared to have something on his mind, but he didn't share it with her. Instead he lifted the magazine. "Maybe I'll see you after the walk."

"Okay." Inviting him to dinner rolled onto her tongue

but she stopped. He'd refused the last two invitations. Three strikes and she'd be out. She lifted her hand in a wave and headed back to the office. This kind of relationship wasn't what she'd wanted. When she took the job at the high school, she anticipated seeing Jonny daily. She'd looked forward to their talks and making plans to do things together as friends.

Friends. The word fizzled. Friendship is what had begun and maybe to Jonny that's what it still was, but to her, their friendship had taken on a new meaning—deeper and fuller. Today again she felt drained. Empty.

An icy chill rolled down her spine. She had to face it. Without Jonny, she felt hollow.

At the end of the school day, Jon slipped into his down-filled jacket, scanned the equipment room to make sure he'd put everything away, and headed for the door. As he opened it, Dale spotted him as he came down the hall and gave him a wave. "You've been quiet lately. What's up?"

"Not much." His mind skipped over Neely to his basketball team. "We're doing pretty good."

"Then why so quiet?" He arched a brow.

"Have I been?" Too much thinking, he suspected, but he didn't know it showed.

"How are those plays we talked about?"

That stymied him. Football yes, but not basketball. He couldn't remember talking to Dale about plays, but then he'd been distracted. "The team's doing great. We've won the last two—"

Dale chuckled. "I was talking about the woman."

"Oh. Right." That resolved his confusion. They had talked plays.

"I thought you'd pick up on that." Dale's smile had vanished. "Not good, huh?"

Jon shrugged. "Could be better."

Dale's large hand grasped his shoulder. "Did you go for the touchdown?"

The coy look on his face made Jon grin, but the situation wasn't a topic to smile about. "I tried, but we've had interference."

Dale cocked his head.

"Her father walked in on us." He closed his eyes remembering. "I could almost taste it."

"Bad luck, but don't give up." He gave Jon's shoulder a shake, and lowered his arm. "One day it will happen."

Jon dug his hands into his jacket pockets. "You know, man, I'm not sure, but I sense her pulling away. She charges forward, and when it looks like a play, she backs off. So I did what I tend to do."

Dale tilted his head, waiting.

"I stepped back. Now I'm sensing her moving in again, and I'm still pulling away. I don't want to be hurt. I've been disappointed before, and I…I don't know."

"It's better to have loved and lost than to never be loved at all. Someone said that."

The quote jerked Jon to attention. Who'd think Dale would quote poetry? "Tennyson said it. I don't remember the name of the poem." But he wasn't sure he agreed with the poet. He'd loved Neely forever, and the ache had never soothed. He tried to toss his feelings off as a teen's infatuation, but now he knew better. Neely had embedded herself into his brain and heart. She would never go away.

"My recommendation. Keep pushing toward the goal. Don't be worried if she heads away from the end zone. You know about fake hand-offs in football. It's part of the game. But it doesn't stop it. It just keeps you on your toes and the game interesting."

Jon blew out a stream of air. “You have more patience and positivity than I ever will in this situation.”

Dale slapped his back. “It’s worth it, pal. Trust me.” He gave him a thumbs up and continued toward the exit.

Jon stood there and watched him go, feeling the sting of his encouragement. He wished he felt as confident about the outcome as his friend.

Outside the wind had picked up and the temperature had dropped. Dark clouds billowed above weighted with rain. Maybe snow. He shook his head, knowing that the walk with Fred would be short or not at all. When he pulled up in front, Fred stepped onto the porch, his jacket and cap on, ready to go. Rather than disappoint him, Jonny locked the car and joined him on the sidewalk.

The conversation centered around sports and the news, but as the wind picked up, Fred grew quiet, and Jon feared the older man was struggling with the walk which could do nothing good for his heart. Jon slowed. “This wind is taking the breath out of me. How about you?”

Fred gave a shrug, but Jon saw the truth in his face.

“Let’s head home. At least the wind will be at our back.” He turned without waiting, and Fred followed. The man’s determination reminded him so much of Neely’s. When the house came into view, the first drops of sleet-like rain hit the ground in large splatters, but he kept pace with Fred, avoiding the desire to run.

By the time, they hit the porch, the rain was turning to snow, and his jacket was drenched. Fred swung the door open and motioned him to enter. “You were right, Jon. Good thing we came back.” He closed the door, his breath still coming in short gasps. “Let’s toss your jacket in the dryer.”

“No. It’s fine.” But before the words left his lips, Fred had pulled the damp jacket from his hands and headed toward the laundry room. He followed as far as the kitchen, concerned about Fred's well-being and now better understanding Neely's constant worry.

He heard the clang of the dryer door and then the whisk of the dryer turning. Fred came through the doorway and headed for the coffeepot. "This calls for something warm." He turned to Jon. "Coffee?"

No point in saying he'd pass. "Sure." Jon pulled out a chair and sat as he watched Fred spoon grounds into the coffee filter.

When Fred turned he leaned against the counter. "I'd like having a son-in-law like you Jon."

He clamped his teeth closed to keep his jaw from dropping. "Thank you, Fred." It was the best response that came to him in the flash of the man's proclamation. "You'd make a great father-in-law."

"You know…" He sank into a chair. "I had those two girls and never had a son. Marion decided no more babies even though I wanted to try one more time. I think a good son-in-law could be the next best thing."

"I think you're right." He studied the man's face, anticipating what might come next.

"Have you ever thought about it?"

Jon's stomach lurched. "About what? Marrying one of your daughters?"

"Neely, naturally. Ashley's seeing Erik, but I'm praying that ends soon. I never liked that boy. He seemed sneaky to me. You're pure honesty, Jon. I've always known that. Your sister is the same. Nice kids. Good parents."

"Thanks. They're still good parents." He held his breath.

"So what about Neely?"

His pulse galloped to his temple and pounded. "She's wonderful, but marriage is something between two people. Both have to be willing."

"Son, I know that. She's a good woman and needs a good man." He faced the coffeemaker and filled two cups. "Here you go."

"Thanks." Jon reached for the mug and saw his fingers tremble. He wasn't opposed to marriage. Far from it. But he feared Fred would put their relationship in jeopardy with his blatant request. If he said anything to Neely, that could possibly end a good thing. He took a sip of the hot liquid and burned his tongue in the hurry to get out of the conversation.

Fred picked up his cup and faced him again. "I suppose I have to leave that up to you and Neely." He searched Jon's face. "But I can pray, can't I?"

"That you can, Fred. That will accomplish more than anything else." He sat facing him, paralyzed.

Fred stepped toward the doorway. "You're right, Jon. Very right."

Watching him step into the hallway, Jon took a deep breath, but Fred turned to face him. "Ever play checkers?" Fred beckoned him to follow.

"Sure have." He walked behind him into the dining room.

"Good. Since our walk was cut short, how about a game?"

He glanced at his watch. Nearly five which meant Neely would be home soon. "Sounds great."

Fred gave him a smile and headed out of the room, he assumed for the checkers, while he sank into the nearest chair, hoping the older man's prayers were given a positive answer by the Lord.

Neely hit the End Call button on her cell phone and leaned her back against the driver's seat. Ashley had phoned just as she'd left the school. The rain had turned to snow, and she slipped back outside, found a scraper in the trunk, and brushed off the flakes that began to cover her windows. Finished, she tossed the scraper into the backseat and settled inside, appreciating the warmth of her heater.

She and Ashley hadn't talked since the recent date with Erik. Her sister bubbled about the great dinner they had and how wonderful Erik had been. The praise curdled her stomach, and Neely had all she could do but to bite her tongue so she didn't make a nasty comment.

Erik knew how to take time to win her over, and then he'd become the Erik she'd learned to face years earlier. He had a knack for maneuvering women to trust him, especially ones who were naive. She and Ashley were both inexperienced when it came to worldly men. Ashley fell in love with Adam in high school just as she'd fallen for Erik. They were young and totally inexperienced.

She learned about life after she got out on her own, but Ashley had married young, and Adam had been her only love. But what could she say? Ashley had already been resentful and accused her of being jealous, and unless she told her the whole story, her sister wouldn't trust her warning. She wished she had the courage to be truthful.

The truth would set her free in a lot of ways. The Bible told her that, too. Though its meaning was different, it still said exactly what she'd faced. If she confessed her lack of virginity to Jonny, it could open doors that she longed to explore. Jonny cared about her and she sensed he cared a lot. She could no longer deny she cared a lot for him, but she feared telling him about her relationship with Erik would undo their friendship, and that was worth too much to lose.

With the thoughts of Ashley and Jonny setting her on the brink of uncertainty, she started the car. As her car rolled down the street, she spotted Jonny's SUV parked in front of the house. She couldn't believe he walked with her dad in the rain and snow, but he was there so they had done something.

She parked inside the garage and entered the back door. Voices came from the front of the house. She slipped off her snowy shoes and dropped her purse on a kitchen chair, then hung her jacket on a chair back and found them in the dining room. "Checkers."

Jonny looked at her over his shoulder. "My jacket's in the dryer, although it's been dry for a while, I'm sure. The weather ended our walk."

A look flittered across his face arousing her curiosity. She sidled closer and looked at him directly. He kept his eyes on the checkerboard as if a Kingship would win him a gold medal. "Who's winning?"

Her father lifted his focus from the board. "Who do you think? Me. I'm the checker champ."

She grinned at his boisterous proclamation. Her father's attitude always improved when Jonny was around to help entertain him. He missed his old cronies, and the awareness triggered her need to get him over to the senior center where he could enjoy some camaraderie.

She slipped onto a chair where she could watch the game, admiring Jonny's wonderful ways with her dad. He appeared to enjoy his company too, and she had a difficult time believing it was an act. Jonny's spirit escalated when he was making others happy. Her admiration grew each time she watched him be the kind of man any woman would be proud to call her husband.

Though the thought encouraged her, the need to tell him the truth dragged her down. Honesty was the best policy. How often had she heard it? Ashley said this very thing. Telling Ashley would be a hairbreadth less horrible than admitting the truth to Jonny. Ashley respected her too, and she prayed Ashley would understand. She kept the idea in mind, knowing she needed to deal with it and make it happen.

"Gotcha." Her father's rousing announcement cut through her concentration.

Jonny chuckled and shook his head. "You sure did, Fred. I didn't see it coming."

Neely studied his face to see if he'd let her father win, but she suspected he was telling the truth. The *truth.* The word dug into her conscience.

"Enough for me." Her father pushed back his chair and rose. "I'll let you two have some privacy." He gave Jonny a look that caused Neely to ponder what it meant.

She waited until her dad left the room. "What was that all about?"

Jonny chuckled. "Does your dad always make sense?"

Not always, but she sensed he was being evasive. "I smelled coffee in the kitchen. Do you want a cup?"

"I had some earlier. Thanks anyway."

She lifted his empty cup and carried it into the kitchen, her mind skittering with questions. As she rinsed the cup, Jonny walked into the kitchen. When she turned, he grinned. "Do you mind if I get my jacket?" He gave a toss of his head. "It's in the dryer."

"Permission granted."

He ambled into the laundry room and came out with the jacket over his arm. "I should be on—"

"Don't run off." The words shot from her mouth.

He eyed her a moment, then dropped his jacket on a chair back. "I thought you'd be busy getting dinner."

Her pulse tripped, gazing into his eyes. "I'm not in a rush." She motioned him to sit, and she pulled out a chair and joined him. "I heard from Ashley, but before I tell you about that, I have something else that's important."

The important reference must have captured his interest. His head shot up and his eyes captured hers.

"The last time you were here you left when the topic of Erik came up. I sensed that you were tired of my preoccupation with him, and I need to tell you that it's not what it seems." Her stomach knotted as the admission spewed from her.

"Neely, you don't owe me anything. I'm sorry if I seemed—"

"You have every right to be tired of it. I'm tired of it, and I think I've made sense out of the problem."

His head raised again as interest grew on his face.

"I'm not interested in Erik. I'm not jealous of his relationship with Ashley. Even she accused me of that. I know Erik too well, and I learned more about him after I'd broken off and moved away. I realized he is a master at manipulation and hiding his licentious ways. He cheated on me, and I'm guessing that's what ended his marriage."

He flinched, and she suspected he knew the truth. Though she waited a moment, he didn't respond. "You know that's true, don't you?"

His body tensed. "I don't like to spread gossip, Neely."

"I don't either. That's why I'm asking the truth."

He looked away, and that answered her question.

"It is true. I see it in your face." The drumming of her heart told her the truth when she looked into his eyes. Now she faced what to do about it.

"My face tells you that much?

"It does." She grinned, and relaxed when she saw him smile back. "So I'm concerned about Ashley. That's all it is. She's vulnerable now, Jonny. This is the first man she's been with since Adam died. She's taking a chance, and he's playing up to her with every ploy he has, telling her how much he likes kids and showing her a good time without expectations. That will change."

Jonny's gaze intensified, and she realized her admission gave away too much. But she'd said it and now she would suffer the consequences. If he asked her, she wouldn't lie to him.

He studied her too long, and she held her breath.

Finally he broke the connection. "I understand, and you're in a spot since she thinks you're jealous."

"That's right."

He reached across the space and rested his hand on hers. "All you can do for the moment is to pray that the Lord protect her, and give Erik rope. If he's the same Erik, he'll hang himself. Count on it. Ashley's not stupid, Neely. She might be naive, but when it comes to being a parent and a woman who enjoyed a blessed marriage, she won't fall for his line. Give her time."

Neely rotated her hand beneath his and wove her fingers through his. "You couldn't have said anything better. I have to be patient and pray that he hangs himself before Ashley's hurt."

He rose and drew her upward. She loved being in his arms, feeling protected and secure. His broad shoulders and taut muscles flexed against her arms. Warmth over his concern eased her fears. She wrapped her arms around his back and gazed into his eyes, more willing than ever to feel his lips on hers. He studied her face, his gaze lingering on her lips, and then drew back. "Patience and prayer is something we all need."

Disappointment rocked her, but before she could take the initiative to act, her dad's footsteps sounded in the hallway. She stepped away as he entered.

He paused and blinked. "I'd say this was bad timing."

She looked at Jonny, and they burst into laughter. The

levity released her stress and reminded her that good things took time. Johnny said it, and he was right. She'd scared him with her wavering behavior, and now if she wanted to move forward, he needed time to trust her. For once she faced what she needed to do, and as she'd realized earlier that day, the truth would set her free.

Chapter Eleven

Neely sat on her sister's living room floor in the midst of miniature cars and trucks while Joey carried on a conversation that partially made sense. When Ashley came from the kitchen with drinks, she shifted toward her. "What's 'kirka'?"

Ashley chuckled. "What's wrong? You don't understand perfectly good English?" She moved her finger in a circle.

She grinned. "It makes sense now." She helped Joey place his vehicles nose to nose in a wide circle. What she wanted to do was ask about Ashley's latest date with Erik, but Joey had intervened with his toys as soon as she walked through the doorway. She hadn't seen him in a few days, and she couldn't resist his cute grin.

"Joey." Ashley's voice cut through his continuing blather. "Let Auntie Neely get off the floor and enjoy her drink."

He studied his mother a minute before he pointed to her pop can. "Drink?" His eyes widened, and she lifted the can and gave him a sip.

Joey turned away, preoccupied by his trucks, and Neely hoisted herself from the floor, and settled on the sofa beside a stack of Joey's books. Ashley read to him each day. She was doing a great job raising her son.

Neely took a long swallow, and settled against the cushion. "Are you doing okay?"

She nodded. "Great. I have another company asking me to do some work at home for them, which is perfect, and I had a great date with Erik." She lowered her head a moment then lifted it with a frown.

Neely's pulse skipped wondering if Erik had done something already.

Ashley ran her finger over the arm of the chair. "I feel somewhat guilty having a good time with a man. I suppose that's natural." She looked up her eyes searching Neely's.

"Erik's the first man you've dated since Adam. I think feeling strange about it would be normal." She studied her but didn't read anything else in her sister's expression. "Erik treats you well? No hanky-panky?"

Her eyes widened. "Nothing like that. He's been a total gentleman. I can't picture him trying anything, Neely. You should know. He was always good with you, wasn't he?"

Neely's blood ran cold, and she look away, struggling with how to respond. Ashley had opened the door for the truth, but saying it aloud weighed heavy in her chest.

Ashley's expression wavered between confusion and certainty.

"Not always, Ash. He was at first, and then he did what he's good at—maneuvering with promises."

"What?" Disbelief filled her face. "You aren't maneuverable, though."

Neely shrank beneath her look. "I was then. Not anymore."

Ashley looked dazed. "I don't understand." Her fingers fiddled with the locket around her neck, one Neely recalled Adam had given her before he left for the Middle East.

Her sister's questioning look put her on shaky ground, and biting her lip to control a rising sob, Neely dug deep and shared her story. As the words left her, relief buoyed the heavy weight of the past and her spirit lifted.

But Ashley's expression pinched as her eyes narrowed. "I can't believe this. You're blaming Erik, and you just admitted the mistake was yours. You thought giving yourself would keep him from dating other girls."

Neely fell back against the cushion. "I was vulnerable. Yes, the mistake was believing that Erik loved me, and that my giving in to him proved my love for him. That's what he demanded." She leaned closed to Ashley's face, her pulse racing. "Do you hear me? Demanded."

Ashley jumped up and the spun around. "I can't believe this. He's the nicest guy. He loves Joey, and he even asked us to Thanksgiving dinner at his house. He's never stepped out of line once."

"Thanksgiving?" She closed her eyes. Erik didn't love kids and Ashley would see that eventually, and Thanksgiving dinner. Her thoughts spiraled. A family day. Erik knew that would grind her, and Ashley had given no thought to their dad. What would dinner be like for him?

"Dad won't mind." Ashley's comment cut through the silence.

She rose and walked past Ashley. "I hope you're right, Ash. I suppose people can change, but he's divorced too, and—" She clamped her jaw. Don't say it. Don't tell her. She thought of all Jonny had said. Give Erik rope, and he'll hang himself. She'd pray for that.

Neely stood in front of the mirror deciding between her hunter green sweater and the camel-colored cowl neck. She choice the latter and slipped it over her head. With her dark hair, she tended to wear gray and maroon, but the camel seemed to brighten her face. Depressed as she had been, she needed something to help her look more cheery.

Her dad accepted Ashley and Joey's absence from their quiet Thanksgiving dinner. Just the two of them. She couldn't call it festive, but at his request, she'd made her mother's sausage bread stuffing, and he relished every bite. She'd heard over and over that it was almost as good as Mom's.

Jonny had felt sorry for them, she was sure, when he invited the two of them to his parents' house for dinner. Rainie welcomed her, too, but it didn't seem right. Maybe she would be invited as Rainie's best high school friend, but Neely's father was another story. She didn't want to put him in that position. When he heard about it later that evening from Ashley who cajoled her in front of their dad for being a martyr—those were Ashley's words—her dad fell silent. Later when Ashley left, after sharing the wonderful day she'd had with Erik, her dad had said he would have happily stayed home while she went to Jonny's family dinner. She wanted to wring her sister's neck for bringing it up.

"You were invited, too, Dad," she'd told him, trying to make sense out of her refusal. They would have been kind and welcomed both of them, but she didn't want to feel beholden. She liked Jonny's parents and they'd always been kind, but she'd felt like the homeless people they'd helped when she was a teen.

She shook her head, wishing the topic hadn't fallen back into her mind. The whole day had depressed her. Now she'd accepted having dinner at Ty's new house—"leftover night" they called it—where they would snack on the day-old Thanksgiving fare and play games. Even this made her feel like a traitor to her dad.

She smoothed the cowl neckline, enjoying the way it fell in almost a square around her neck, and headed downstairs.

When she entered the living room, the TV blared as her

dad looked up from the paper and grinned. "Now, don't worry about me. I can see that look on your face."

She shook her head. Everyone seemed to read her mind. "I wrote the telephone number on the pad in the kitchen if you need me." She took a step toward him and then paused. "Should I fill a plate of leftovers for you? That's easy, and you can pop it in the microwave."

"Neely, I lived alone a long time after your mother past, and you've only been here three months. I can make it on my own for a few hours." He reached for her hand and gave it a squeeze. "Now have a nice time. I like that boy, you know."

"I know. You and Jonny get along great." She slipped her hand from his, knowing that soon he'd be recommending she propose to Jonny.

Before he said anything, car lights flashed across the wall. "He's here." She stepped to the closet and pulled out her coat. Before slipping it on, she gave her dad a peck on the cheek. "Don't wait up for me."

He shook his head, a grin growing on his face. "Like old times."

The doorbell rang, and as she opened it, she remembered how her dad always waited up for her. Never her mother.

Jonny stood on the porch, snowflakes caught in his hair. He shivered. "Ready?"

She nodded. "See you later, Daddy." She wiggled her fingers his way.

Jonny grasped the door, and leaned in. "Good night, Fred. I'll get her home safely."

"I know you will." Her dad's voice sailed toward him.

She stepped onto the snowy porch and closed the door, and Jonny linked his arm in hers as they walked down the stairs.

"You missed a good meal." He leaned his shoulder against hers. "And I missed you being there."

"Thanks, but we had a nice dinner at home." Nice but quiet. She told him about the stuffing her father loved and Ashley's visit. "But it turned into a mess. Can you believe Ashley called me a martyr because I stayed home with Dad?"

He opened the car door, and she slipped inside. Jonny rounded the car, and when he climbed in, he paused. "Your sister feels guilty leaving you and your dad on Thanksgiving. That's her way of putting the blame on you."

He was probably right, but it hurt. With Christmas coming, she'd have to plan differently. She didn't want the same thing to happen again, and it could. This time she'd accept the invitation…if he asked this time.

As Jonny drove to Ty's, they talked about the food they planned to prepare for the homeless, but again she recalled the feeling she had about the dinner invitation. Silly that she'd felt that way. His parents' invitation had been natural. How many times had she eaten with Rainie and Rainie, with her. Maybe she had played martyr.

When they pulled into the driveway, Neely gazed at the lovely house Ty had recently purchased for Rainie for their first home. The glow of lights in the windows and the welcoming porch light aroused Neely's envy. She wanted the best for Rainie, and she would have it with a great husband. Ty had proved to be a hard worker, intelligent and loving. He made Rainie laugh, and as her dad always said, "Laughter is the best medicine." She'd learned that over the years. If she can laugh at her flaws and foolishness, she felt better. Her biggest folly with Erik was one thing she could never laugh away.

Jonny opened her door, and they made their way through the snow to the house. Ty opened the front door, a warm greeting on his face that almost matched the warm glow through the windows. "Welcome to our leftover night."

She chuckled as Rainie wrapped her arms around her and drew her in. The scent of baked ham permeated the air, and she realized she'd forgotten to eat lunch. Ty swept them into the dining room. "I'll take your drink order, and just dig in. Everything's ready."

Neely accepted a cup of hot mulled cider and the others gave their orders, and she stood at the buffet beside the plates and gazed at the lavish meal. Rainie slipped to her side. "Mom insisted we bring half the dinner here for tonight. You know her."

Neely did. She took a slice of ham, candied yams, traditional bread stuffing, mixed vegetables and coleslaw. The others followed along the buffet, and they settled around the table. The conversation between bites lifted her spirit—memories of their past, wedding plans in the spring, and Jonny's winning basketball team. Rainie asked about her job at the school and about her dad, but she noticed no mention of Ashley entered the talk. Jonny must have warned Rainie. Her heart skipped thinking of Jonny's protection. Like a fairytale hero, he'd taken on the job of dragon slayer.

When Ty finished, he gathered dishes and gave them a list of board games they could play. While he and Jonny talked the pros and cons of the games, Rainie hooked her arm into hers. "Let me show you the house. I can't wait to move in."

The men's voices faded as Rainie led her to a cozy den and then the year-round porch that looked out into a well-landscaped backyard. Next she followed Rainie up the stairs to the bedrooms, and once inside the master suite—huge walk-in closet and large bathroom—Rainie pulled her down on the edge of the mattress and grasped her hand. "I've never seen Jon so happy."

Her chest constricted as she looked into Rainie's eyes, having no idea how to respond. "He's a nice guy. I can't imagine him being any other way."

But the look on her friend's face made her question what she'd said.

"He's been a loner in a way. Jon's always cordial to people, and they like him, but he doesn't always relate. He sticks pretty much to his class work and his teams. He's very responsible."

"And caring. He treats my dad as if he were his own." After the words came out, Neely wished she hadn't spoken them aloud.

"I know. It's you, Neely. You bring out the best in him."

She flinched. "I don't do anything special. Nothing. I'm just me. We see each other at work. He enjoys exercising. He likes my dad. He—"

"He likes you. He always has. Why do you think he followed you around so much when we were teenagers? He swore me to secrecy. I always wanted to tell you to be gentle with him. He adored you…for some reason."

The last phrase lightened the mood, and Neely chuckled. "Thanks."

"I'm teasing. I love you, too, but his love is real." Rainie locked her eyes with hers. "I'm not joking now."

Air seeped from Neely's lungs. "He told me a while ago he had a crush on me when—"

"It's was a crush…but it's not a crush. It's real feelings. I see it in his eyes. The way he looks at you. The things he's been doing with his time. Walking with your dad. Do you think that's typical of a man? Sure, he likes your father, but he's spending time with him."

"I know. I wonder why."

She dropped back against the mattress and gazed at the ceiling. “Then you’re stupid.”

Neely blinked. The past few months she didn’t know anything about herself. She’d become a martyr. A worrier. A blind person. Just plain stupid if what Rainie said was true. “But I didn’t know. I thought…”

“Has he kissed you?”

“He tried a couple of times.”

“Tried?” Rainie’s forehead rumpled.

“My dad walked in on us.” Neely reeled with the memory.

“And that’s it?”

Neely’s heart flew to her throat. “Once, but it was short. Dad again.”

“Your dad? Jon ought to drag you away by the hair to a quiet, private place…like a caveman.” Her frown deepened. “It was all one-sided then?”

The truth will set you free. The meaning tore through her mind. “No. I kissed him once when his team won the homecoming game.”

Rainie’s head shake went along with her arched eyebrow. “It only counts when it’s on the lips.”

“It counts.” She couldn’t help but grin.

“Hey, what are you two doing?” Ty strutted through the doorway with Jonny on his heels.

“Girl talk.” Rainie rose. “I guess we have to play games.”

Ty slipped his arm around her back and drew her close. “I’d say so.”

They chuckled as Ty kissed the end of her nose.

Even that sent Neely’s pulse soaring. She stole a look at Jonny and realized he’d been gazing at her. He closed the distance and slipped his arm around her waist. “I talked him out of Monopoly, but I gave in to Clue. Can you handle it?”

"Sure. Miss Scarlet committed the crime in the library with the candlestick."

He squeezed her closer. "I guess you can handle it?"

Rainie's words wrapped around her mind as she headed down the stairs. Thinking back so much made sense, and even though Jonny told her he'd had a crush, she didn't know the depth of his feelings. For that matter, she didn't know the depth of hers.

In Jon's eyes the Thanksgiving weekend had been an amusement park. Neely's refusal to his dinner invitation sent him on a roller coaster ride. He knew the car would nosedive down a track flying through a dark tunnel but never sure of when. Though he'd enjoyed his family, his thoughts had been tied to Neely. She'd told him about Rainie's invitation to spend the day with Erik, and it seemed a perfect chance for her to spend time with his family. He even considered Fred's part in it. His dad would have talked a leg off the man who was hungry for adult male conversation. He adored his girls, but men's talk and women's talk was decidedly different.

But Neely had refused. Asking her out for Friday took courage. He anticipated the same kind of response. Instead he'd enjoyed a pleasant surprise. The evening had been fun, good food, good talk, and lots of laughs playing the games. Neely looked relaxed, and her eyes sparkled when she discovered a clue that allowed her to solve the first game. Mr. Mustard did it in the conservatory with the rope. Hearing her pronouncement made him smile.

He'd longed to kiss her many times when he observed the loving relationship between Rainie and Ty. They were meant for each other, and in his heart, he believed that Neely was meant for him. Now to convince her.

One thing that confused him was the end of the evening.

She and Rainie seemed to have an unspoken conversation, and the more they eyed each other, the more she relaxed. He'd noticed her looking at him for no reason, and he sensed something was going on in her head, but he couldn't figure it out this time.

Neely had even taken his hand and gave it a squeeze when he'd said what a good time he was having. It was her way, he guessed, to tell him she was having fun, too.

He'd wanted to ask her out tonight, but she'd dropped a hint that she wanted to spend time with her dad since she'd been away from him the night before. More guilt, he figured. So why hadn't he made plans with her dad? Then he'd be there whether she liked it or not. He grinned, listening to his cockamamie thoughts.

Instead of moping, Jon turned on the TV and leaned back in his recliner. Since she'd said no about dinner, he planned to eat light. It made sense following the abundance of the Thursday and Friday meals. He'd pulled out a can of low-cal soup—the brand all the women had been talking about in the teacher's lounge the past few weeks—and picked up a turkey sandwich.

He snapped through the channels, searching for one of the college football games. He clicked past Oregon at Stanford and grinned when he landed on Michigan at Ohio State. He eyed the clock and decided to wait awhile before eating.

Flipping up the recliner footrest, he leaned back, remote in hand. The TV commercial ended, and the camera focused on the replay as the announcer relived the touchdown.

His cell phone buzzed, and he snapped the chair forward, wondering where he'd put his cell phone. He slapped his hands on his pockets, then dropped the footrest and darted to the table across the living room. Neely's ID glowed on the screen. He poked the button. "Hi. This is a surprise."

"I hate to bother you, but can you come over?"

Her voice rang with panic. "What's wrong?"

"My dad. I'm not sure what's going on and he's refusing to let me call a doctor. I hate to call Ashley and ask her to come. She has Joey and—"

"Neely, stop. It's okay. What are his symptoms?"

"He seems short of breath, and he's holding his chest. He says he's nauseated. When I ask if it feels like a heart attack, he rolls his eyes and saying it's nothing."

He could picture Fred denying what was evident. "Pains down his arms?"

"I asked. He said no."

"No sense in fooling around. I'll be there in a minute. Don't listen to him. No one wants to be sick. Call nine-one-one."

Sandwich forgotten, Jon slipped on his shoes and coat, grabbed his keys and darted from the house. He prayed Neely did as he said and called an ambulance. As he shifted into Reverse, guilt assailed him. Should he have made Fred walk slower and pause to take a rest? He'd heard him huffing and puffing at times, but he knew exercise could strengthen muscles, and the heart was a muscle. But maybe he'd made a mistake.

If he'd been at fault, he'd never forgive himself.

Chapter Twelve

"I'll have to ask you to wait in the waiting room for now. It's right down the—"

"I know where it is." Neely stepped toward the triage curtain.

The doctor's assistant nodded and waited as Neely slipped into the space between the closed curtains and made her way to the triage exit. She could hear tears and sobs, slurred curse words, and the hum of voices dealing with the emergency patients.

Stepping into the admittance area, she drew a ragged breath, longing to calm her fears. Guilt riddled her that she'd allowed her dad to do things she preferred he didn't. She'd read the internet article on heart attacks and thought she'd done the right thing.

She turned down the hallway, and while struggling to regain her composure, she entered the waiting area. Jonny rose as she approached, and she stepped in his arms. "I'm so worried. I pray he'll be okay."

"Prayer is good for a start."

His words whispered against her ear, sending a chill down her spine. He held her close, and the scent of his aftershave wrapped around her, offering a feeling of comfort. Jonny provided her with a sense of security she hadn't felt in years. No matter what she needed, he seemed to be there for her. "Thanks so much, Jonny."

"What are they doing now?"

His serious expression touched her. "After they checked his records, they gave him nitroglycerin, but the pain didn't stop. They did an EKG and blood tests while I was there, and now I think they said they wanted to do an echocardiogram. Maybe chest X-rays, too." Feeling overwhelmed, she sagged against him.

His arms loosened, and he motioned to the chairs. She unwrapped herself from his arms and sank into a Naugahyde chair. "I had to leave. I wish I could stay and hear what they say."

"The doctor will send for you. They'll talk to you. I'm sure you know that." He slipped his hand over hers as she gripped the chair arm.

"I know. We brought my mom to Beaumont when she became so ill. I remember it all too well." She lifted her eyes to his. "I'm sure that's why I'm so frightened."

"But you don't have to be. Your dad's coloring was good, and he was spunky. You know how he is." He gave her fingers a squeeze.

For the first time since she'd called him, she grinned. "He can be a pistol, can't he?"

Though Jonny grinned back, she sensed something more in his expression.

"You're worried, too."

"No, I believe he'll be fine. If it is a heart attack, he's here and in good hands. You were on top of it, and we got him here fast."

She lowered her head, hating to admit what had been bugging her. "I shouldn't have let him do so much. I shouldn't have believed the articles."

He chuckled, and it surprised her.

Jonny lifted her fingers and kissed her knuckles. "You're saying what I've been thinking. I'm the one that went walking with him. I heard his labored breathing sometimes, but I didn't stop him because I know exercise is good for heart patients. He wasn't walking up hill. He—"

"Stop blaming yourself." Her chest tightened. "You're sweet, Jonny."

He grinned. "Thanks. I guess I feel a little to blame, too."

They settled into comfortable silence. The TV blatted a game show, and she studied the question, digging in her memory for the answer.

Jonny rose and stretched. "Want some coffee?" He motioned to the urns close to the door.

She nodded, all the while fearing the stuff would taste like mud. Surprised when he came back, she took a sip, and the coffee tasted fresh. "Thanks." She settled her back against the seat cushion, willing her mind away from her worries. Sending up a prayer, she closed her eyes and pictured her dad's face. Jonny was right. He had color in his cheeks, and the pain didn't stop him from his usual comments about the Bible saying honor your father, and she wasn't because she was forcing him to go to emergency. Jonny had stood beside her chuckling, and she caught her dad giving him a wink.

He loved Jonny. She saw it in his actions and heard it in his comments, especially the continual reference that she should snatch him up before another woman stole him away. Those times she did think about the possibility. She'd watched Cindy throw herself at Jonny more than once, and she guessed Cindy wasn't the only woman in Jonny's life who saw him as a possible husband.

When she looked up, his gorgeous eyes captured hers,

and her lungs collapsed. He would make an amazing husband. Anyone would be a fool not to see his great attributes.

"Five bucks for your thoughts."

She chuckled at his playful request, but behind her grin, heat rolled up her chest to her cheeks. Had her eyes given away her thoughts? "I wouldn't tell you for a hundred dollars."

"Whoa. Those must be some powerful thoughts." In a heartbeat, his grin shrank. "I know you're thinking of your dad."

True. She had been, but as happened so often, Jonny elbowed his way into her mind and everything else scattered. She checked her watch and then compared it to the wall clock. "How long do you think we'll have to wait?"

He shrugged. "Hard to know how long the tests take."

The time could drag on forever, and she faced that she should have insisted Ashley come with her. "I'm sorry I dragged you into this. I should have—"

"You should have done what you did—call me." He slipped his arm along the chair back and drew closer. "Ashley has Joey to handle. Bringing him here would be hard on her and you."

He was right and yet… "When I called to tell her we were taking him to emergency, she just said keep her posted."

"See. She has more sense than you." He gave her a poke.

The lighthearted moment settled around her, and she elbowed him in the side. "Thanks." Then she shifted to face him. "I really mean that. Thanks for keeping me steady and from going off the deep end, and thanks for your help always. I've come to count on you for so many things, and…" And what? And I should stop? No. She couldn't. He'd become a third arm, someone she couldn't imagine living without.

He shushed her. "I'm here for you because that's where I want to be."

His words washed over her as Rainie's comments floated beside them. "I've never seen Jon so happy. You bring out the best in him."

But was she the best for Jonny? A shiver ran down her spine. She wanted to be, but did Jonny love her? The question had stayed in her mind after talking with Rainie. Jonny, the boy, had faded from her memory. The living, breathing specimen that she looked at now had taken over her mind and heart. But she'd nearly driven him away with her constant reminder of the past.

Dumb. Dumb. Dumb.

"Don't try to fool me."

Jonny's voice cut through her mental acrobatics.

"Those thoughts are worth millions."

"You're right." She managed a smile while her emotions see-sawed. But more and more, Jonny made her feel good, and she was learning to accept this.

Turning her eyes toward the TV offered her an escape from Jonny's gaze, and that would be the only way she wouldn't fall apart between worries about her dad and her amazing feelings for him.

He lowered his arm between her and the chair, his fingers brushing her arm, his touch as gentle as grass bending in a breeze. They both quieted, she in her own thoughts and an occasional distraction from the TV. Time ticked away, and the longer she waited the more tense she became.

Jonny drew her closer, and she responded by resting her head on his shoulder and closing her eyes. When Jonny shifted, her eyes opened, and she realized she'd drifted to sleep, a defense against the tension that wrought her.

"I think the doctor's at the door."

She looked up as he gazed her way and beckoned. "Jon." She rose and grasped his hand. "Come with me."

Though he hesitated, his face touched by surprise, he did as she asked and followed her to the doorway as the doctor stepped into the hallway.

"Was it a heart attack? How is he?" The words shot from her mouth before she'd given him time to speak.

The physician grinned. "His heart looks stable. No changes. Nothing to worry about there, but he does have a serious problem with GERD. He has—"

"GERD?" Her eyes searched his.

"It's gastroesophageal reflux disease, and it's aggravated by your father's hiatal hernia."

"Hernia? I didn't know." Her head spun with health issues she hadn't anticipated.

"Apparently he didn't, either." The surgeon gave her a tender smile. "Let's go into the conference room while I explain what we'll do." He motioned to her to follow.

She grasped Jon's hand and pulled him along to catch up with the doctor.

"We're starting your father on some medication to soothe the acid reflux, and then he can go home. I'll give you scripts for the medication he'll need to take daily and some tips on keeping him healthy."

Her pulse skipped. "He can come home?"

A grin grew on his face. "He can, and he certainly let me know that's what he wanted."

If he hadn't grinned, she would have sunk through the ground. "Daddy speaks his mind."

"I noticed."

Jon squeezed her hand as her worries melted. Her dad would be okay. She hadn't done anything wrong. She looked at Jon and saw relief on his face as well. She could tell he felt as she did—grateful.

* * *

Jon knew something had changed with Neely, but he wasn't certain what it was. First she'd called him Jon. That was a first, and though he loved the idea that she realized he was no longer a kid, the name sounded odd coming from her. Although sometimes in the past, she let down her guard and related to him as if they were more than friends, other times she seemed to flinch when he touched her. He'd learned to not take her reaction to mean she disliked him but that touching her stepped beyond the line of their relationship. Today gave him hope. Jon. He'd get used to it.

As the snow fell, drifting into crystal piles against the pharmacy's brick, he waited in the car with Fred, who'd fallen asleep in the backseat, while Neely ran in to pick up her father's script that would control his excessive stomach acid. The physician had explained what happened to cause the problem. Avoiding alcohol and smoking didn't affect Fred since he didn't touch either, but eating large meals and eating before bedtime was a problem. Fred liked food. And he didn't like to be told what he should eat. Now Neely had a new problem. The image brought on a grin, and he could almost hear Fred's barbs and picture her frustration.

Neely appeared in the doorway and slipped into the car, an RX logo on the white paper bag she carried. She glanced into the backseat before she spoke. "Now, to get him to take these capsules daily and to follow the other suggestions." She released a sigh and shook her head. "I love challenges." She rolled her eyes.

"Maybe the resistance won't be as bad as you think." He checked the review mirror to make sure Fred was still sleeping. "He didn't enjoy the feeling he had from the heartburn. The pain is awful, I've heard. That should encourage him. But give him a chance to follow the doctor's orders before getting after him."

"Getting after him? I don't do that." She drew back. "My dad—"

"Listen to the man, Neely."

She twisted and as she did, he saw her father gazing at her with one eye open. "See if I can follow the doctor's suggestions before you have a tizzy. And you do get after me."

"Daddy, I—"

He leaned forward and grasped the seat back. "Be honest, Jon. Does she?"

Jon grinned at her and gave a shrug. "Yes, sometimes."

"There. This nice intelligent young man knows the truth."

Though Neely appeared cornered, she shook her head and didn't try to rebut the accusation. Her orders for her dad were out of love. He knew that. And her concern flavored much of what she did. He saw it in her face and her actions.

She remained quiet for a few minutes, and he avoided starting any new topic before he was assured she wasn't angry at him. When she shifted toward him, tension had faded from her face, and she sent him a weary smile. "I want to get dad a new pillow, a firm one to put under the one he loves. That will boost him up. The doctor said it reduces heartburn by allowing gravity to repress the acid reflux. They have wedges for that purpose, too."

He closed his mouth realizing no other topic would be possible until he got her home and her father settled. Focusing on traffic, he listened to his mind play her voice over in his head. Jon. Jon. He'd longed to hear her call him Jon for so long, and now, he asked himself why.

Neely stood in her bedroom, getting a grip on herself. The long day had worn her out. She felt transparent, and she struggled with what had happened between her and Jon. She sucked in air. She'd called him Jon. The name had slipped from her, and the look on his face set her reeling.

She had no idea what he thought, and Neely didn't want to talk about it because she had nothing to say. They'd been quiet in the car after her father had awakened, and grateful for the distraction, she let his presence put a barrier between her and Jon's conversation. His eyes flashed a warning that he wanted to know what caused the change. She could not tell him without letting him know how she felt.

She'd realized, finally, that his feelings for her had grown—really grown to more than a childish fixation. If she faced the truth, his kiss had told her the same thing, but she'd wanted to deny it. A woman four years older than a man felt awkward. Older men and younger women seemed acceptable, but the other way around caused different reactions. Cradle robber? Worse yet, a cougar. Is that what she was?

Strangely, she didn't feel the difference in age. Jon—Jonny—her heart zinged hearing the familiar nickname. Jon's behavior balanced her own. They enjoyed similar interests that were ageless. When she saw their reflection in a window or mirror, age lost its importance.

She sank to the edge of her bed and slipped off her shoes, replacing them with her fuzzy slippers. Pressing the palms of her hands against the mattress edge, she hoisted her body upwards, feeling the weight of the fearful day. But God had blessed her dad and given her hope that he would live a long life if he took care of himself.

The question that still clung in her mind hadn't been answered. With that in mind, she bounded down the stairs and found him in the kitchen nosing in the refrigerator.

"Hungry?"

He glanced over his shoulder. "What do you think?"

She grinned. "Where's Jon?"

"Dying of starvation too." He turned to face her and shrugged.

The question nudged her again. "What did you eat for dinner yesterday, Dad?"

"Leftovers."

She nodded and opened the refrigerator. The turkey breast she'd baked looked as if it hadn't been touched since Thanksgiving. She eyed the container of mashed potatoes and it looked full. She spun around. "Daddy, what did you eat for dinner yesterday? Didn't you have the turkey?"

"Didn't need it. I was too full." He evaded her eyes.

She closed the door and strode to his side and waited until he looked at her. "What did you eat then?"

"What do you think?"

Her patience skittered away. "This isn't a guessing game. Dad?" She sensed Jon's presence and glanced toward the doorway. He leaned against the jam. She turned again and focused on her father. "What did you eat?"

"The stuffing."

She pictured the large casserole she'd made. She opened the refrigerator and it was gone. Unbelieving, she opened the dishwasher and saw the empty dish inside. She spun around. "You ate the rest of the sausage stuffing."

"It was your mother's best recipe." He grinned. "And you make it as good as she did."

His grin didn't soften her frustration. "Do you realize

how many of those ingredients are on the danger list for acid reflux? Grease from the sausage. The spices in the meat." She gave Jon a pleading look. "No wonder you were sick. I'm surprised you didn't burn a hole in your stomach." She wanted to scream. Leave him alone for one evening, and look what he did.

"He didn't know he had a problem with GERD, Neely. He knows now."

Jon's soft voice swept across the space.

She eyed her father who gave Jon a smile. "Good answer, son."

"Hold on, Fred. I'm not excusing you. You're an adult and know you should eat healthy foods. Did you have a salad? Vegetables?" He didn't break eye contact with her dad.

Neely's focus shifted from her dad to Jon and back again.

"I thought you were on my side." Her dad pinned Jon with his gaze.

Jon strutted across the room and lapped his arm over her dad's shoulder. "Did I ever tell you that I learned where your daughter inherited her stubbornness?"

Her head drew back. "Stubborn?"

"Determination, I meant." He gave her a sly grin.

She couldn't subdue her smile. In the processes of his comment, her father had forgotten the argument. "Jon, would you like to eat with us? Please?"

"When you put it that way…but only if you let me help." He strode deeper into the room and stood beside the counter.

She put him to work on a salad while she rewarmed the two-day-old ham and potato leftovers minus the sausage stuffing. Her father slipped into a kitchen chair, watching them as a look of pleasure stole to his face. "You two look like a married couple."

They spun around at the same time, Jon and she each holding a knife. His head pivoted from one knife to the other, while they burst into laughter. The look on her father's face was priceless. Before anymore was said, Ashley's voice came from the living room, and she entered the kitchen with Joey in tow. Neely could barely find him bundled beneath the scarf, cap and gloves in which her sister had dressed him.

"Hope I didn't scare you." Ashley set Joey on the floor, and he grasped a chair leg and pulled himself up. "Papa." He grinned at her dad and waddled around the table, his arms extended. When he landed on grandpa's lap, he scanned his surroundings and opened his arms again. Neely reached toward him, then realized his eyes were on Jon.

"Hi, pal." Jon scooped him up into his arms, and gave him a hug as Joey eyed the salad bowl and then turned to check out the ham.

"Mama, I hungry."

Ashley shook her head. "He ate an hour ago." She pulled out a chair, and sat across from their dad. "How did things go at the hospital?"

While he told Ashley his side of the story, Neely glanced at Jon who had a grin on his face. They both shook their heads. Though he veered away from his guilt with the sausage stuffing, her father told her the details, and when he finished, she pulled the mashed potatoes from the microwave and popped in the ham.

"Join us?" Neely shifted her eyes from her sister to the refrigerator.

"No, Erik said he'd call about tomorrow. He wants to take Joey to the park to play in the snow."

Neely pulled out a dish of applesauce from the fridge and

eased around. "That should be fun." An opposing comment fought to escape but she squelched it. Erik would hang himself just as Jon had speculated.

As she placed the food on the table, Ashley kissed their dad and scrambled to catch Joey who had headed into the hallway. She leaned back in and gave a wave. "Glad you're doing fine, Dad. Take care of yourself." She eyed Neely. "If you need me, call."

Neely nodded, thoughts flitting around the latest news. Erik had planned a day in the park with Joey in the snow. She really wanted to see that.

Keeping her mouth closed, she settled at the table beside her dad and Jon, and folded her hands. When the sound of the front door closing signaled Ashley's departure, she bowed her head and said the blessing. But part of the prayer she kept silent. Ashley needed protection, and the Lord had the power to do that.

Chapter Thirteen

Talk about determination, today Jon charged his purpose with it. He wanted to talk with Neely one way or the other. She'd missed church to stay home with her dad to watch what he ate. She'd promised not to make comments or give instructions unless necessary, but he questioned whether it was possible.

He told her he'd drop by following the service, and he stepped out and grasped the church worship folder. Maybe the lessons would lift her. She needed inspiration. He could see that. Her worries about her father and other secret fears that hung over her had affected her behavior. He hoped today the sunshine would peek from behind her gloom.

Instead of Neely, Fred answered the door. He gave his head a tilt toward the kitchen. "She's talking with Ashley." He closed the door and gave a shrug. "Something happened. She's been on the phone for fifteen minutes with hardly a peep out of her except an occasional word or two."

Not wanting to interrupt, Jon sat with Fred and chatted about the weather and his health. Not much had happened since yesterday, although something must have happened with Ashley. Finally his curiosity won out, and he rose and wandered to the kitchen door. Erik's name was the first comment he heard, and when he stepped in further, Neely looked at him over her shoulder and covered the mouthpiece. “He stood her up.” Following her whisper, she rolled her eyes. Although he wanted to grin, he didn’t. He mimed a rope around his neck, his head dangling to the side, and she gave him a thumbs-up.

As he pivoted, thinking he’d heard enough, Neely ended the conversation so he stopped and turned back. “What happened?”

“She waited and waited for Erik to get there. After an hour and no call, she took off Joey’s snow pants and jacket. He cried because she’d told him they would make a snowman. Now she’s upset too. I still hear her making excuses though. It’ll take more than this for her to learn the truth.” Her expression reflected her unhappiness for Joey more than the pleasure of Erik showing his true self.

He rested his hands on her shoulders. “Want to take them to the park? I make a mean snowman.”

She eyed him from head to toe. “You’d do that? You don’t have the right clothes.”

“My boots are by the door, jacket on the closet doorknob, and I have scarf, hat and gloves in the car.” He tilted her chin upward. “I’m ready.”

She gazed down at her jeans and grinned. “I’ll call Ashley. Let’s meet her at Geary Park. It’s close, and it even has swings and slides.”

“And snow.”

Her face brightened with her chuckle. She hurried back to the phone, and in moments, she darted up the stairs and soon came back down again wearing a warm sweater and boots. From the closet, she slipped on her blue down-filled jacket, wrapped a red-and-blue scarf around her neck, pulled on a knit cap in the same color and grasped red knitted gloves. He grinned at her color coordination even for playing in the snow.

As they parked along the street by the park, Ashley's sedan pulled up nearby. Neely jumped out and hurried to her sister while he grasped his scarf, cap and gloves. He locked the doors, and strode toward them.

He grinned, seeing Joey so bundled up he could hardly stand. When the boy saw him, he waddled to his side, his arms open in an embrace. Jon swooped him up, hearing the boy giggle and squirm in the air. The sound caught his heart. One day he might be a father. A wife by his side and a son or daughter would complete him.

A hand touched his arm, and he turned. Looking into Neely's eyes, his chest constricted. She could complete him. Her gaze drew him in and he felt lost in her eyes. Ashley's voice broke the spell as they turned in her direction.

The sun glinted off the fresh snow like crystals on a wedding dress, a picture recently embedded in his mind. Pure, fresh, beautiful. His gaze slipped to Neely who had followed Joey into an open stretch of snow, and he watched her showing him how to form a snowball.

Temptation overcame him as he scooped up a handful and formed it into a weapon. Instead, he headed for an open area and added a larger handful of snow to the smaller ball and began forming the base of the snowman. When he looked up, Joey and Ashley were searching for limbs and rocks to form the face and arms of the snowman. Neely caught his eye and headed toward him.

"She's not saying much about Erik, but I can tell she's already forgiven him." She lowered her head and shook it. "I fear she's going to be hurt, Jon."

He straightened his back and slipped his arm around her shoulders. "You can't protect everyone, Neely. They have to learn for themselves. That's what you've done all your life, haven't you?" He had an ulterior motive for his comment, but he thought it fitting.

She searched his eyes and nodded. "I've learned more than I would have believed." She looked away for a moment before she faced him again. "Even now."

"We all do." They looked at each other, eyes searching each other's face and the meaning seemed clear. Neely had grown and changed. Something had made her see him differently, and he thanked God for the new awareness. Now, he prayed she might realize she couldn't live without him. He lifted his head toward heaven. Was that asking too much?

Joey's giggles sailed across the stillness. He forced his mind back to the snowman, and when Joey toddled to his side, the boy gave the snowman's bottom a big hug. "Help me, Joey."

The boy dropped the three stones he'd held in his hand, and joined Jon pushing the next snowball across the snow, watching it gain in size. When it was ready to hoist onto the base, Jon moved Joey to the side and lifted the heavy white ball. While he and Joey rolled the snowman's head, Neely and Ashley bolstered the snowman for stability and shoved in the arms—two mismatched tree limbs but it was better than nothing.

When the head was attached, they let Joey add the last stone for the other eye and they stood back while the boy clapped his hands, his grin long and his cheeks rosy.

"Who wants to go down the slide?" Jon clapped his hands and Joey headed toward him, but tripped over his too large boots and landed on the ground. Not a tear, he laughed again, and Jon wished he could be as joyful when he tumbled over one of life's too big problems.

Ashley stood at the bottom of the slide while he lifted Joey to the top and guided him down the snow-filled incline. His giggles filled the air and made Jon laugh, too. When he turned to Neely, he found her seated on a swing, too small for her, but she looked cute.

Ashley's cell phone played its melody, and her focus shifted to the call. Joey wiggled, wanting to be let go, and Neely came to his rescue while Ashley continued her conversation. When she clicked off and turned around, her face glowed.

"Erik?" Though Neely tried to cover her sarcasm, he heard it on the fringe of her question.

Ashley nodded, her cheeks glowing. "He said he loved me." She gazed at them as if she expected a cheer, but neither said a word, and Ashley's glow faded. "He had a family emergency, but he'll come by tonight after Joey's in bed."

Jon clamped his mouth closed, longing to send out a warning, but Erik would give himself away just as he suspected.

With the excitement of the visit, Ashley gathered Joey in her arms and gave him a kiss. "It's time to go home, sweetie."

"No, Mama." He kicked his feet, but the kicks did no good.

Ashley gave a wave. "Thanks for joining us. It was more fun with you here." She pointed toward her car. "We need to head home. I want to have dinner and then get—" she pointed to Joey "—to bed."

Neely waved back without a word, but he added his concern. "Take care, Ashley."

She only grinned and hurried to her car.

When he turned and looked at Neely's face, he knew what he had to do. She'd be upset for the rest of the night if he didn't try to make her forget. He sprinted away, formed a powdered snowball and flung it at her.

She ducked, but it hit her cap. "Rat." She bent down and grasped a mitt full of snow, forming a ball as she ran toward him. She gave aim and as he swung around, she hit him in the back. He pivoted and dragged his glove through the snow as he headed toward her. She tried to run, but he caught her and slipped the snowy glob down her back.

Her scream scared birds in the trees, and they took flight as he caught her in his arms before she could grasp her ammunition. She wiggled and slipped her boot between his, tripping him up. He stumbled backward and she threw her weight against him, and he plopped into the billowy snow with Neely on top of him. She slid sideways, and he held her tight before she could wrestle away.

Their eyes met, anticipation rushed through him, longing to tell her how he felt and to feel her lips against his. Neely stopped struggling and braced her hands against his chest, her gaze adhered to his. He arched his back, raising himself and drawing her into his arms. Their lips met, firm and eager. No hesitation. No withdrawal but giving and loving. He opened his eyes and looked at hers, half-lidded. They eased apart, connected by the moment.

She drew in a breath. "Jon, I—"

He shushed her. No excuses. No apologies. No Fred. This kiss had been part of God's plan.

At work, Neely avoided Jon. He'd tried to talk with her after they'd returned home on Sunday, but she said the exercise wore her out, and she didn't invite him in. She saw the disappointment on his face. Her reaction had nothing to do with her feelings for him. She'd faced weeks ago that Jon had gotten under her skin, deeper than any other person in her life, but she didn't know what to say to him and until she told him about her and Erik, she had no idea where their relationship would go. That scared her.

The kiss lingered on her lips that day, and even today, she could still feel the pressure of his mouth, the warmth of his lips on hers, and she'd allowed her own feelings to exceed the depth of her emotions that she'd worked so hard to contain. He knew she hadn't backed away from the kiss. No matter what she did or said, the feelings she had for Jon influenced her every waking moment in one way or another.

What she needed was courage to talk with him about Erik, but telling her sister had only caused more harm than what she'd intended. She'd expected her sister to rally round and agree that Erik had taken advantage of her naïveté. Instead, Ashley had concocted a twisted view of her being the one to take advantage of Erik. Now her confidence about Jon's reaction see-sawed.

Her trip to the lounge to warm her lunch undid her avoidance during the morning. She knew Jon had classes at the other end of the building, and she thought he had lunch later, but she'd timed it wrong. When she opened the door and walked in, he sat at one of the round tables talking with his friend Dale.

She gave a quick nod and headed for the microwave, but the brief acknowledgment only made her avoidance more obvious. Before she could heat her soup, Jon strode to her side and slipped between her and the doorway. "I don't know what's wrong, Neely, but I know something is."

She shrugged. "I'm okay."

He studied her face a moment, then gave his own discouraged shrug. "Did you remember we're supposed to cook for Welcome Inn tonight?"

His reminder punctuated her foolish behavior. She and Jon's life had bonded. She couldn't walk past him as if they'd just met. "I forgot, Jon."

"But you can make it?" Question glinted in his eyes.

The look weakened her attempt to find an excuse. "Yes. What time?"

He told her the time and menu. "I'll pick you up. It's on my way."

"Okay. Thanks."

He gazed at her and the beep of the microwave saved her from being caught by his probing eyes. She lifted out the container and closed the door. "I'll see you later." Before he could say anything more, she swept past him and strode to the doorway. She didn't look back.

In the hallway, she stood a moment, trying to make sense out of her behavior. After analyzing her feelings and digesting the truth about their relationship, fighting it was as useless as kicking at stones. She had done nothing wrong, and neither had Jon. They'd kissed, a mutual expression of their feelings. They couldn't hide it anymore. She'd resolved her antiquated attitude over the age issue. At least, she thought she had, and now only one thing kept her from being open and accepting the love that Jon offered her.

But her teenage discretion lay on her heart like a boulder. If it had only been once, she could explain it away, but she'd given in to Erik's sexual conquests repeatedly, always wondering what was supposed to be so wonderful about the act. To her it only left her feeling stained.

Those were times she wished she had a mother she could have talked with, one who would provide her with answers and soothe her guilt—even if she'd been able to talk with Ashley, but Ash already had her sights on Adam, and she prided herself on staying pure for him. Purity was no longer an option for Neely. But now she remained as close to pure as was possible until the time when God blessed her union with someone…if that would ever be.

She might have been stronger if she had understood how Erik had deceived her. Love didn't have to be proved in the way he demanded, or any way, for that matter. Love proved itself by its unselfishness, concern and thoughtfulness. Love opened doors of the heart offering tenderness and giving while wrapping every fiber of a person's body and mind with fortitude and faithfulness. What she had with Erik had not been love. She'd given in to his lust and had been a victim of her own ignorance.

She carried her soup back to her office, and having lost her appetite, she delved into her work and willed the day to pass quickly.

Jon stirred the red meaty sauce and stole glances at Neely as she grated cheese for the lasagna casseroles. Periodically she stepped beside him to eye the noodles, adjusting the temperature and giving the pasta a stir.

They'd talked briefly but not about anything important. With others in the church kitchen, conversation of importance wasn't possible, but he refused to leave her this time without dealing with the crazy things going on in their relationship.

He'd weighed the idea of dating someone else and seeing if that triggered a change in Neely's attitude, and even though Cindy came to mind, he again rejected the idea as unkind and impossible. He would have been miserable and if Cindy did have feelings for him, he would have hurt her, and who knew if Neely would have reacted or not. Her behavior left him in a muddle and seemed beyond understanding. He wondered if she understood herself.

Since she'd begun to call him Jon—which still sounded strange coming from her—he'd assumed the age difference and their past relationship had faded in her memory. So he suspected that wasn't the issue holding her back.

The kiss he'd longed for made him weak. The feeling embarrassed him, and he would never admit it to anyone.

His lungs had collapsed, his pulse fluttered like a moth drawn to light, and his heart pounded. He suspected those descriptions were found in romance novels and not reality, but he couldn't deny he'd felt every crazy sensation with her lips against his. Even the icy ground warmed with her touch.

Mad man. He'd flipped. Lost his mind. No, he'd lost his heart.

Gathering his wits, he turned the burner to low, then stepped away from the stove and strode to her side. "Need any help with the cheese? The sauce is ready, and I suspect the noodles are al dente."

She arched a brow, a slight grin touching her mouth. "Al dente."

"I know a few classy cooking words."

She chuckled and set down the grater.

He watched her stand beside the pasta and give one noodle a test. "You're right. If you drain these and rinse them with water, I'll bring the cheese over to the work table."

He followed her instructions, and they stood at the table, layering sauce, noodles and cheese into six casseroles while others in the room where making chicken and rice casseroles and one was baking cookies. Giving to others had touched Jon since he was a kid, and he'd recognized the same value in Neely.

Sometimes he asked himself if their mutual interest in charities had been the attraction, but he negated it, recalling that he loved her banter. Her quick rebuttals and playful digs didn't hurt him but made him feel worthy of her time. Pretty ignorant when he thought about it, but maybe not so after all. Here she was in his life again.

When the casseroles were constructed, he popped them in the oven, and thought about a place they could go not too far away to find privacy to talk. He preferred to be somewhere else without people nearby, but what could he do?

"Jon." One of the women who seemed to be in charged approached him and stopped to check the casseroles. "Nice job." She smiled at them. "Let me know what time they can come out of the oven, and I'll see they get into the freezer when they're cool enough. No sense in waiting that long. I have to be here anyway." She waved her arm toward the exit. "Now you two get out of here and have fun."

She smiled, and he smiled back, thanking her for the offer. Hope rose, knowing they could leave the building. Neely followed him to the coat rack where they slipped on their jackets and headed into the frigid night air. Once inside the car, he turned the key and as the engine sounded, he adjusted the heater. They sat a moment, letting the defrosters work on the windows.

When the wipers swept away the moisture, he turned to her, and when he spoke, he heard her voice echoing the same words. "We need to talk."

Her eyes widened, and they laughed. He eased sideways. "Sounds like we've had the same thing on our minds." The kiss? The relationship? He hoped it was both.

"I think so." She looked uneasy, but he decided it was shyness rather than discomfort.

"Here or should we go someplace? I have cocoa at home."

"Hot chocolate sounds good."

He backed from their parking spot and pulled onto the highway heading home in silence. She leaned back in her own thoughts while he moved words around in his mind, deciding what he wanted to say and how he wanted to say it.

The ride was short, and once inside, with the hot chocolate ready for their cups, he poured the drinks and guided her into the living room. His fireplace had been converted to gas, and he turned it on, pleased that he'd purchased a quality insert with flaming logs that glowed along with glowing embers and ash.

Neely sank into a chair near the fire and curled her legs beneath her. She watched the flames lick the logs and then faced him. "It looks real. Amazing."

He thought she was amazing. "I like it. Sometimes it's difficult to tell what's real and what isn't."

Her brow flickered with question. Then a coy grin stole to her lips. "Is that an innuendo? I suspect it is."

"It does relate to life, don't you think?" He hoped she accepted his attempt at a lighthearted comment.

Her head lowered, she nodded. "Jon, you're right. What's real gets lost sometimes in what's in our memory and in our imagination. Even if we suspect it's real, we doubt it because it's not what we expected or what we think it should be."

"Memories can fade, and imagination can stimulate." His chest constricted watching her struggle with her words. "I told you a few months ago that I had a teenage crush on you in high school. That memory never faded."

Her head pelted upward, her eyes searching his. "But the feelings faded."

"Not really. It slipped into hibernation waiting for spring. Spring came last August when I saw you on the football field." A weight fell from his shoulders releasing the words he'd wanted to say for so long.

"You feel the same way now?"

He shook his head. "No. That was a boy's crush on the first girl that aroused his awareness."

"Oh." She lowered her head again.

"Now my feelings are man size, and it's no longer a crush. It's much more than that."

Her head inched upward. "My mixed up thinking lasted for a long time. You know that."

"I do."

"And then it grew into a nightmare."

He tensed.

"But like nightmares, I woke up. I began to see the man and his wonderful attributes. The past faded. I admitted it the day I dropped the name Jonny and called you Jon."

He nodded, praying what she said next turned out to be as wonderful as her present confession.

Her eyes searched his once again. "You've become important to me. You're someone I can count on and whose companionship I enjoy."

But what about love? "You're important to me, too. Very important." He waited.

She remained silent, and the longer he waited, the crazier his pulse responded. "So what does this mean?" He held his breath.

"I think..."

The wait dragged on, draining his patience. "You think what?"

"I think...we should see where it goes."

Where it goes? It wasn't what he wanted to hear, but it was better than what she might have said. "Okay." He shuffled the idea around, trying to make something practical out of it. "Do you want to continue as we have been? I'm not sure I like that idea."

Her face paled. "I..."

This time he wasn't going to provide suggestions. He needed to know what she wanted, but as time ticked away, he had to bite his tongue to keep from speaking.

A sigh rattled through her. "I think we should date. Real dates, not just you dropping by."

"Dates, but not dropping by. Is that it?"

She looked confused. "I do like you to drop by. So does Dad." Her gaze drifted to the flicker of the fireplace, and he noticed her rub her arms as if chilled. "But I'd like to have a real date. You invite me to go somewhere and tell me what time you'll pick me up."

His ribs pressed against his heart. "A real date, but I can still drop by."

She nodded, a childlike look flooding her face as if she had a secret hiding place but couldn't tell him where it was yet.

He closed his eyes, thanking God for the progress. He had a secret he couldn't tell her yet, but one day he hoped he could say the words that he'd said over and over in his heart. He'd loved her forever.

Chapter Fourteen

Neely sat in her room after Jon brought her home, weighing what had happened. The long awaited discussion had risen as slowly as yeast in dough, but warmed by their recent kiss, it could no longer be contained. It swelled into the open. Their voices melded into one as they introduced the need to talk, not a new topic. During their times together, they had insinuated the need, and Jon had at least tried to open the door. She had closed it with a kick.

Jon's patience with her humbled her. He'd put up with her wavering attitude, her drawing close and pulling back—not because she wanted to, but because she couldn't control her anxiety. But they'd talked, and now the door had opened to stay until one of them closed it forever, or they met in the opening and removed the hinges.

Her limbs tingled with the realization of her commitment—excited but apprehensive. Questions filled her mind, and the one question—how she would explain her lack of chastity to Jon—raked through her over and over.

She needed validation, but again she didn't want to drag Ashley into it. Too much tension had formed since she was dating Erik. She might see it as an attempt to make him jealous which was as far from the truth as she could get.

Before Erik happened in Ashley's life, she'd encouraged her to look at Jon with different eyes. But now her own eyes had cleared, and Ashley had been right. If her feelings for Jon wasn't love, she didn't know what was.

Faltering, she remembered that she'd once thought she loved Erik. Was love that fickle or were the amazing sensations and thoughts filling her now proof that she truly loved Jon?

Neely slipped on her pajamas and bathrobe and tiptoed down the stairs. The house had quieted, and she assumed her father had gone to bed. At the bottom, the light reflected from the living room, and she wandered in.

"Daddy?" She approached his chair, waiting for him to wake. Her stomach knotted when he didn't move. "Daddy?'

He bolted upward, his eyes glazed with sleep. "What's all the yelling?"

Laughter and tears mixed. "You scared me. I thought—"

He dropped the leg rest and shook his head. "That I'd died. Nope. Not yet. The good Lord still has work for me here."

She settled on the edge of the sofa. "Work? What kind?"

"Female." He grinned.

She studied his face, trying to make sense of his meaning.

"Don't look dumbfounded." He waved his hand toward her. "You and Ashley."

"We're fine, Daddy." She realized he could take her comment wrong. "But I'm glad you're still with us."

"I'd like to see both you girls settled. You know what I mean?"

She could guess.

"Ashley needs a husband for that dear little Joey. A good husband who loves her and will care for her and their family. She's been strong, but that's not the way a young mother should live. Adam would want her to find someone to love her again."

The romantic words washed over her. She'd never pictured her dad in that light. He and her mother obviously had two children, but other than that, she'd never seen a sign of closeness or affection. Her mother had cooked and cleaned. Her dad had worked and handled the yard and house maintenance. The bills and two children seemed all they had in common.

"I'd like that for Ashley, too." But not Erik, and she suspected her father's emphasis on good husband meant he longed for her to find someone else. "What do you want for me? A good job?"

He tilted his head, searching her face. "The same. A good husband, a family and lots of love."

Tears sprang into her eyes, and she looked away before he noticed. She brushed them with the back of her hand. "Anyone in mind?"

He chuckled. "Oh, girl, you don't have to ask that question. You already know the answer."

"You think a lot of Jon, don't you?"

"Love him like a son."

Son. Two girls and her dad had never had a namesake or anyone to carry on the Andrews name. "What do you think of the two of us?"

"Makes me happy." His gaze captured hers. "And it makes you happy. No denying it."

"But what about the age?"

He drew back. "Age? Neely, you're old enough to get married if that's what bothers you."

A laugh sputtered from her before she could contain it. "I meant our ages. I'm four years older than Jon."

"Four whole years. Let's see. When you're seventy-five, he'll be seventy-one." He shook his head. "That is scandalous."

Her chuckle returned. The way her dad said it made her concern sound stupid. Maybe it was.

"We've agreed to date."

He studied her a moment, his face serious, and then he slapped his knee and broke into a guffaw. "My word. What have you been doing all this time?" He held up his finger, his laughter growing. "Babysitting?"

The situation tickled her until she cried. She reached her father's chair, sat on the arm and leaned down to hug him. "Daddy, I love you."

"I love you, too, my girl. You'll work it out. It's what the Lord wants. I sense it."

Her pulse tripped. "You think so?"

"Positive. Jesus and I are good friends. He tells me everything."

She rested her cheek against his, praising the Lord for a parent who was so filled with love and faith, it made her almost burst.

"Joey." Neely turned around and listened. She'd agreed to babysit for a couple of hours while Ashley went Christmas shopping for Joey. She guessed Erik was involved. He'd do anything to convince Ashley he loved kids and solidify her forgiveness for missing their date.

Every time she talked with Ashley, Neely made it a point to avoid discussing anything about her relationship with Jon and no judgments at all about Erik. She kept her mouth closed.

She never considered watching Joey as a task. She loved the time spent with him, but she learned quickly a bright almost three-year-old was a handful.

"Joey?" She darted through the house and found him in the laundry room, trying on her boots.

"Go outside." He poked his finger against the storm window where the snow drifted in large flakes.

The boots nearly swallowed him. "You need your own boots, sweetie." She opened her arms and he rose, half wearing one of her furry Mukluks.

She knelt down and pulled her boots from his legs, helped him push on his own, and then reached for his snow jacket and maneuvered his arms into the sleeves. When she reached for the zipper, it slipped from her hand as he jerked away and beat against the door. "Doggie."

She followed the direction of his finger and saw a black lab. "It's a doggie, sweetie." She turned him toward her again and slid the zipper upward.

Her phone jingled from a distance. She'd left it in the living room. She suspected it was Ashley wanting her to keep Joey a little longer. "Hang on, Joey."

She bolted from the room before Ashley gave up and grasped her cell phone, but when she checked the ID, the caller was Rainie. "I thought my sister was calling." She relayed her reasoning.

Rainie agreed. "When Erik and Ty are together, I overhear some of his tales and shake my head. Ty tries to overlook his exaggerations and his preoccupation with conquering the woman he dates. I really don't know why they're friends, but I guess when Ty was first getting involved in his business, Erik jumped in with some financial support and led him to a great lawyer who's been an attribute. Ty sees the good side of Erik that you don't see and I question."

The conversation veered from Erik and segued into Rainie's purpose for calling. A wedding shower was in order, and she'd agreed to host it along with another friend so details needed to be workout. "How about this weekend? Maybe we could get together Saturday and make some decisions. See if Shana can make it. I think we can get a lot finished then."

When they'd made plans, except to check with Shana, Neely hung up and realized she'd left Joey alone too long. When she reached the laundry room, it was empty. Her heart dropped. "Joey."

She checked the kitchen, downstairs bathroom, guest bedroom, everywhere. "Joey." Her voice sailed up the stairs with no response. "Joey! Please." She closed her eyes, her lungs depleted of air. Gasping, she grabbed her jacket from the hall closet, slowed long enough to grasp her cell phone, and raced to the back door. When she opened the storm door, tiny boots imprinted the snow and at the bottom, dog paw prints bounded from one direction to another.

She covered her face, sending up a prayer. "Lord, I can't believe I was that stupid."

The flakes had grown larger and the footprints were nearly lost in the snow. She spotted a boot mark here and a dog print there, but once she reached the sidewalk, she stood, tears blurring her eyes. Finally she sighted the boots at the edge of the street and inches away car tires embedded in the new fallen snow.

Kidnapped. No. Please, Lord. No. "Joey!" Her voice pierced the air. Fingers shaking, she flipped open the cell phone and punched the speed dial. When she heard his voice, she sobbed. "Jon. I need you. Please help me find Joey."

He didn't wait for her to explain. His own panic evident, the call ended, and she followed the car tracks as far as she could, but the falling snow and heat from traffic turned the pristine flakes to mush. Her finger hovered over 9-1-1. That's what she should do, but her mind raced to find a reasonable answer that didn't include Joey being abducted. Calling the police meant— Common sense prevailed, and she hit the emergency numbers, sobbing her story to the dispatcher.

When she ended the call, the snow had lessened, and only a few flakes drifted from the sky, but the street left little evidence she could pinpoint. Not willing to give up, she strode down the curb and searched the ground for clues. Anything to help her know which way he'd gone. Which way the car had gone. As she scanned the distance, a vehicle moved down the street. A stranger? Police? Jon? When it neared, she recognized Jon's SUV, and her pulse escalated, her throat trying to swallow the rising sobs.

Jon turned into her driveway, jumped out and ran to her side. "Did you call the police?"

She nodded, and as she explained what happened, his eyes searched the road. "Let's walk." He slipped his hand in hers. "Look for fresh tracks on driveways."

That thought hadn't crossed her mind. Jon's hand left hers, and he pointed ahead. "Let me check." He darted to the door and knocked. When a man answered, she saw Jon's shoulders slump, and he turned her way and shook his head.

She tried to catch up with him, but he hurried on. Finally he turned and pointed as he bounded up the sidewalk, flew up the porch steps, and rang the bell.

Before she could reach the house, Jon came through the doorway waving one arm with Joey in the other. Her stifled sobs broke free as she ran to meet them.

"Joey, Auntie couldn't find you." She threw her arms around him. "Please, Joey, don't ever—"

"You cry?" He touched her cheek, and the warmth of his hand followed her rivulet of tears.

She withdrew his finger and kissed it. "I thought

you were lost. Please, don't ever go outside alone. Your mama—"

"Doggie." He swung his hand over her shoulder, and when she looked to where he pointed, she recognized the black lab wagging his tail in the doorway.

Jon slipped his arm around her. "Your neighbor had just called the police. She said he was beside the street with her lab, and she knew he was too young to be out alone so she took him inside to keep him from..." He nudged her.

When she looked up, a police car had pulled to the curb, and a young officer stepped onto the street. "You found him."

She nodded. "I'm so sorry to have troubled you. My nephew—"

"Ma'am." He shook his head. "That's our job. I'm glad this one has a happy ending. Sometimes they don't."

Fighting more tears, she nodded. "I know. I'm grateful to my neighbor who did the right thing. I want to thank her."

He gave her a gentle nod. "Next time, big guy, you wait until your mama can take you outside. Okay?"

Joey grinned. "Okay." Then he swung back toward the neighbor's door where the black lab still watched, wagging his tail. "Doggie."

The officer gave her a wink. "Keep an eye on him."

A ragged breath blasted from her chest. "Absolutely, and as you can see, I have a big job."

He took a step backward, gave her a faint grin, and strode to the patrol car. As he pulled away, she handed Joey back to Jon. "I want to thank the lady, and Jon, thank you, too. You're the first person I thought to call. I don't know what I'd do without you." Her heart rose to her throat, gazing into his clear blue eyes. As she turned, the reality of her words struck her. Truly, what would she do without him?

* * *

Jon leaned against the chair back and hit his cell phone speed dial. A grin stretched his cheeks, and he couldn't stop the silly expression. Neely asked for a real date, and tonight he was taking her up on her offer. Helping her find Joey had opened the door for a non-planned visit. Only now could he be lighthearted about the event that had frightened him more than he wanted to face.

He couldn't imagine being a father and realizing his toddler was missing from the house or the yard. When he heard Neely's frantic call for help, panic had raced through him. Relief had rendered him useless when he found the boy. Tears filled his eyes, and it had been years since he'd cried. He never wanted to experience anything like that again, and he thanked the Lord it had a happy ending.

Afterward they talked about the scare and agreed when dealing with a precocious toddler, an adult should never walk away. They'd learned their lesson, and Ashley forgave her since Joey had done the same to her.

Four jingles. Neely usually answered on the first couple of rings, and he lifted his finger to end the call, then heard her hello. "Hi. This is Jon."

She chuckled. "I know. Your number and photo came up on the screen."

He knew that too, but how did a guy open a conversation to ask a girl on a date? It had been so long. "This is sort of last minute, but I noticed a folk rock program at AJ's Music Café tonight, and I thought it might be fun."

Silence.

Hmm? "Would you like to go with me?"

She snickered through the telephone. "This is a date."

"Right."

"What time?"

He shook his head, loving the going-out part but hating

the game. "The music starts at eight. I'll pick you up at seven forty-five."

"Want to come earlier?"

His head flopped forward, swinging from side to side. He felt like a teenager.

"I made Dad's favorite poppy-seed cake, and I think you'd like it. Plus Dad likes to talk with you."

"Cake and your dad. Can't go wrong with that." He smacked his palm against the side of his head. The conversation sounded forced. He liked the old way. If Neely wanted to date him, that's what they'd do. "How about seven?"

She agreed, and he hung up, tossing his head against the chair back and closing his eyes. A date meant they had to go somewhere. He liked sitting around talking, making hot chocolate and laughing at the crazy things in their day. It had nothing to do with spending money. He never considered himself cheap, but going out for the sake of going out seemed...weird. That's the only word he could think of.

Between dinner and watching the news on TV, he got through the late afternoon and early evening. He stood at his closet weighing decisions between slacks and a V-neck sweater over a sport shirt, khakis and a knit shirt or going even more casual in jeans and a sweater. He had no idea what Neely thought was appropriate attire for a date, but to be safe, he chose the khakis. Sort of middle ground.

His meal set like a ten-pound weight on his stomach. He loved the naturalness of his relationship with Neely—like two people who'd been married a few years, still loved to explore their relationship, but wallowed in the comfort of a dear friendship. Too bad romancing had to lose the positive qualities of friendship.

The question hung on his mind as he dressed and did a

final check in the mirror. He paused. Maybe it didn't have to. All he needed was to call and invite her to spend the evening at his house. Sometimes she'd invite him there. Once the invitation was accepted, he could forget the date aspect… Maybe not forget exactly. Flowers once in a while, a card on her desk at work, things women enjoyed. Even men liked surprises. Nothing wrong with that.

His buoyant exit from the house calmed him. If he could calm himself—be natural, don't think date—then everything could remain the same. He hoped.

When he pulled into Neely's driveway, he sat a moment, reviewing what he'd thought before he left. He'd always been confident once he'd matured. He grasped reality and bounded up the sidewalk, noting that someone had shoveled snow for them. He hoped it wasn't Fred. That was not part of his approved activities.

After ringing the bell, he waited only a second before the door flew open and Neely stood in the lamplight, a smile warming her face. She pushed the door back. "Come in. I'm making Daddy tea. Would you like some?"

He preferred coffee but he could tolerate tea. "Sure."

She nodded as he slipped off his coat and draped it on the doorknob, knowing they were leaving soon.

When he stepped into the living room, Fred grinned at him from his recliner. "Good to see you, Jon."

He looked as if he had something on his mind, but was it only his imagination? "Good to see you, too, Fred."

Since Neely had vanished, he settled into an easy chair, assuming she'd be arriving with a piece of cake and mug of tea for him and her dad.

Something seemed strange, and he realized the TV wasn't blurting commercials and game shows. Instead soft jazz music swept across the room, subtle yet there. An antsy sensation slid through him.

"Nice music." He uttered the words into the air, not knowing if Fred knew jazz from blues from pop rock.

"I remember when Brubeck and Ahmad Jamal were popular. Did you ever hear Jamal play blues?" His eyes seemed lost in memory. "It was great."

"I've heard some. I enjoy blues." Pleasure spread over Jon, learning something new about Fred. The love of music filled his body, and he eased into the recliner like a man warmed by his wife's kiss on a cold winter's day.

"It warms the soul."

Neely stepped through the doorway. "What does?"

"Blues." He really saw her for the first time that evening. She'd worn jeans. He grinned. Jeans with a pullover the color of rust. She'd pulled her hair back with a copper-colored clip but a few wispy ends brushed her cheek, and he longed to smooth them away and feel the softness of her skin against his fingers.

"I like blues and jazz." She motioned toward the CD player. "Can you help me, Jon?" She beckoned him to follow her into the kitchen.

"Sure." Relieved, he rose, gave a nod to Fred and followed her.

When he came through the doorway, he noticed a tray with mugs and pieces of cake, but he also observed the look in Neely's face. "What's up?"

She glanced away.

He held his breath.

"Would you mind not going out tonight? Dad's been talking about you stopping by, and something's going on with him. I hate to leave."

"Chest pains?" Jon searched her face.

"No." She sent him a tender grin. "His spirit, I guess. He's melancholy, and that's not like Dad."

Jon drew closer and opened his arms. "I'm happy to

stay here." As if she'd heard his wish, he wrapped his arms around her.

She rested her head on his shoulder. "I'm being silly, I suppose, but I thought maybe we could visit with him a while or—"

"No reasons necessary." Now the soft music made sense. "I've always enjoyed visiting with your dad and just spending time with you."

She tilted her head upward, her eyes searching his as if seeking affirmation that he really meant what he said. Her soft lips tempted him, and he lowered his mouth to hers, drawing in her sweetness. She yielded to the kiss, her head moving slowly as if to the rhythm of the soft melody floating from the living room.

When she lifted her head, she didn't look away. Her eyes sought his, and this time, she moved forward to touch his lips again with hers as naturally as a bud opening in spring. He held her tighter, his heart expanding as if wanting to draw hers in. He thanked the Lord for her, for the difficult times and the good ones, allowing him to see the joy of God's blessing.

They parted but lingered in their embrace before she smiled. "Do you like cold tea?"

"For this, I'll take no tea. Nothing but you."

A tinge of pink rose to her cheeks, and she squirmed away. "I like this dating stuff."

If it meant kisses like this, he did, too. He pressed his hand to her cheek as she drew back.

"Anyone for a game of rummy?"

Her dad's footsteps sounded near the door, and Jon stepped away as her father came into the kitchen. "How long does it take to make tea?" His gaze drifted from him to Neely as a grin grew on his face. "I know, sometimes things take a long time. And then, they're ready."

Jon chuckled and shook his head. Fred knew more than they did. He grasped her dad's shoulder and gave it a squeeze. "You're a smart man, sir."

"Not really. I just use my eyes." He glanced at Neely a moment. "And my heart."

Neely's face brightened. "You've always used your heart, Daddy." She turned to face Jon. "So does Jon."

He didn't know what to say since thank you didn't seem a good response to that kind of compliment. He opted for changing the subject. "I've always enjoyed rummy. That was one game my parents allowed us to play."

"Marion didn't like games." He seemed to slip away, his eyes distant.

Jon waited to see if Neely would respond. She didn't.

Fred looked up. "Now that I think of it, Marion didn't like a lot of things."

Neely's eyes widened, and she flashed a look at Jon, as if questioning her dad, too.

He decided Neely was right. Something was going on in her dad's head that neither understood. Although in that fleeting moment, he remembered that Fred had experienced a health scare. Maybe seeing death at his door for those hours made him look at the past with new eyes.

With everything that had gone on between him and Neely, new eyes seemed what they all needed.

Chapter Fifteen

Neely ended the call and rose from the edge of her bed, her head pounding with questions. Since she'd admitted her feelings for Jon and verged on shouting it to the world, her father's recent melancholy and her sister's resent vicissitude had thrown her happiness into the shadows. Nothing made sense anymore.

Since Erik came into Ashley's life, her sister had presented an upbeat attitude, but beneath it, Neely sensed something wrong. When she'd telephoned a few moments ago, Ashley had slipped and admitted that Erik had stood her up again with a promise to take Joey to a puppet show at the library. Neely recognized another avoidance tactic she attributed to Erik.

Trying to cover her disappointment, Ashley had defended Erik as she often did. "If Adam hadn't died, he would have offered Joey every opportunity to expand his world, and I accept that Erik doesn't have the same connection with Joey." She'd paused before she added, "I'm sure Erik will in time."

Neely's experience with Erik nixed that thought.

With that still in her mind, her thoughts slipped back to the following Thursday when her father's distraction had bothered her. He wasn't a daydreamer, but she sensed that he had slipped into a kind of melancholy that he couldn't push aside. Even today, something bothered him, and she wanted to find out what was wrong.

Though she'd kept her mouth closed with Ashley, she couldn't with her dad. His health issues motivated her. She strode down the stairs, and at the bottom, she heard him rummaging in the kitchen. "Hungry, Daddy?"

He shrugged. "Bored mostly."

"Nothing on TV?"

He curled his nose. "Nothing I want to see."

"Then let's talk." She beckoned him toward the living room.

He scrutinized her a moment. "Do I have a choice?"

Though she almost grinned at his typical response, she took it as humor. "I don't think so."

She headed for the sofa, hearing his footsteps behind her. After he plopped into his chair and brought up the footrest, she studied him a moment. "Something's bugging you. Are you worried about your health?"

He shook his head. "I suppose the heart attack scare made me think, but I'll be happy being with the Lord so it's not that. No fear of dying." He grinned. "Anyway, I figured I was fine, and I went along with the E.R. visit for you."

"Really?" She arched a brow, but from his expression, she accepted that he was telling her the truth. "You were talking about Mom last Thursday when Jon was here. Are you still grieving, Daddy?" It had been four years, but grief had a way of sneaking back into a life. She'd recognized it in her own experiences.

"Not the kind of grief you mean. I'm fine. I suppose thoughts of death roused some old disappointments, but nothing you can fix."

A different kind of grief? She'd come home to fix things

if they needed fixing. Then she thought of her mother. "You mentioned Mom didn't like a lot of things. What did you mean by that?"

"My big mouth." He shook his head and looked away. "Nothing. Just a thought."

"But it's a thought that's bothering you."

"Girl, you are bugging me. You don't need my old rambling thoughts. What ifs and should haves aren't healthy or helpful. That's the past. Let it lie."

She scooted forward toward the edge of the sofa cushion. "No. I can't." She leaned closer. "Do you know why?"

He shook his head.

"Because I love you too much."

He drew in a ragged breath. "I love you that much, too, Neely. I…" He shook his head. "I wish your mother and I could have shown it more."

"It wasn't you, Daddy." They'd reached the root of the problem. Finally. "You know Mom didn't have it in her. She was different."

"And I knew that when I married her." He sent her a tender smile.

"You did?" She couldn't hide the surprise in her voice.

"How could I not know? Your mom had a difficult time when she was younger, and I hoped my love could change her." The smile vanished, and he drifted away again.

"But you couldn't."

He didn't respond, but he didn't have to. She knew the answer. "Why? What had Mom gone through. If I understood, it might—"

"Your mother never talked about her problems, Neely. She didn't want to rehash them, and I respected that. Don't ask. I don't care how determined you are. Don't ask me."

She'd never seen this side of her father. His voice held the kind of determination she'd been teased about, but this was no joking matter. He meant what he said, and she clutched her hands together, willing herself to hang tight and not push. Today pushing would only create a rift between them.

Neely rose and sat on the arm of her father's chair, resting her hand on his shoulder. "I love you, Daddy, and I'm sorry I asked." She leaned over and kissed his cheek.

He pressed his palm against her fingers. "No need to apologize. I'm sorry you girls were cheated out of a strong mother's love, but she loved you the best she could." He patted her hand, and they sat in silence while she thanked God for the bond they had.

No words needed to be spoken. Secrets were secrets, and this one died with her mother. Maybe one day the answer would come. Maybe not.

Jon started the car and turned on the heater, then gathered the packages from Neely and put them in the trunk with his own.

Snow had covered the ground and layered the trees, leaving the street a pristine backdrop for their Christmas shopping. She had gone to church with him on Sunday, and they'd collected names from the Giving tree. He'd picked one for a man who needed a winter jacket and boots. Necessities. He enjoyed giving things they needed. Neely had selected a little girl who also needed a coat, but she'd added a potholder maker and two coloring books and crayons. He grinned, picturing her selecting the items as carefully as she might have chosen them for herself.

But that hadn't been the end. She'd noticed the mitten tree, which included gloves, scarves and knit caps. In the stores, she'd gone through numerous racks matching colors and making sets even though she knew the sets would probably be broken. She made him smile.

As he reminisced, he brushed snow from the windows, his feet slipping beneath him in the flaky piles. Snow and Christmas went hand in hand.

When he finished, he brushed snow from his hair and shoulders before opening the car door. As he slipped into the seat, he tossed the scraper into the back. "Good job tonight."

"It was. I liked this date."

When she grinned, he couldn't help but chuckle. "Me, too." In the short time she'd brought up the idea of dating, he'd learned that dates to her had a different definition than it did for many women, and that difference was one of the things that made him adore her.

She slipped off her gloves and held her hands toward the warmth coming from the car vents. "Does this all seem silly to you?"

"Shopping for the needy?" He couldn't believe his ears.

She looked at him as if he were an idiot. "The whole dating thing."

"Not anymore."

She loosened the base of her seatbelt and shifted sideways. "Explain."

"The first night I came over for an official date, I felt uncomfortable. I didn't know what you expected or what I had to do. Does that sound odd?"

"Nope." She pressed her lips together, but he saw smile lines beside her mouth.

"Explain." She'd finagled a response from him so why not try it with her?

"I didn't know what to expect either, and the more I thought about it…" She shrugged. "It didn't exactly make sense."

He kept his eyes on the traffic, but he longed to look at her.

"We've been comfortable together the way we were and

why add another element. I like the casual fun we have. I love that you entertain my dad. He needs that so much, but I don't want you to feel you must."

"Neely, you know better than that. I care about your father, and I get a kick out of him. He's different from my mom and dad, yet he's the same in a way." He glanced her way. "He loves his kids, and he wants the best for you all."

"My mom was unlike other mothers, and I really want to know more."

As she continued, Jon heard the story of the cryptic comment of her father. He understood why she longed to know what had happened to her mother, but he doubted she would ever know. Her dad could be as bull-headed as she was. "Does it really matter?"

In his peripheral vision, he saw her study him a moment.

He sought a better question. "Would it make any difference?"

"Not now. I can't be more empathetic, because Mom is gone, but I might feel better."

"Some things we'll never know until we see God face-to-face, and then will it be important? I think we experience things in our lives that we might never understand, but from them we learn and change."

"I've grown in patience." She gave him a crooked grin. "But I have a lot more to learn."

"As long as you and I are changing for the better, we're making progress. Even today. This talk."

"You're smart, Jon."

"It's easier to be smart about someone else's issues than to be intelligent about your own."

She plopped back against the cushion, her body looking more relaxed. "I want to give us a chance, Jon. I might as well be open. I know I've been wavering and foolish at times, but besides being determined—as you always remind me—I'm scared."

"Of me?"

"No, silly. I'm more comfortable with you than anyone."

His pulse tripped. He wanted to ask her to repeat it again to make sure he heard her and not just his wishful thinking.

"I'm not sure why I question everything. Maybe it's the influence of my mom, but I'm not sure. When I loved her, I didn't get what I wanted in return. Do you understand?" She pressed her fingers against her lips as if she were holding back words or her emotions. "I wanted a mom like yours. One that made cookies and laughed with your sister and me. If we had questions, she'd answer us with the patience of a saint."

A twinge of sadness worked through him. "I didn't know that, Neely."

"My dad was the one who tried to be that for us." A grin broke through her thoughtful expression. "Except for the cookies."

"We'll excuse him for that."

"We will."

He'd turned down her street, and when he pulled into her driveway, he turned off the lights but left the car running. He unbuckled her seat belt, then his own, and when she loosened her arms, he drew her to him. "One of these days all of these particular worries and questions will be unimportant. The only thing right now that's important to me is you."

She tilted her chin upward, and he lowered his lips to hers, wrapping himself in the bliss of a relationship that had made a sharp turn and was heading home. Home to the heart of the matter.

Through the wide front window, evening darkened the sky. Neely rose and flipped the switch bringing life to the miniature tree lights. Ornaments rousing many memories hung on the branches, and she stood a moment taken back to her youth before she returned to her spot on the sofa.

With the distraction, Joey's eyes widened, sparkling with glee as if he had never seen a Christmas tree. "Light." He pointed to one of the glistening crystal bulbs.

Jon chuckled and chucked him under the chin. "You like those pretty lights, don't you?"

Joey's head bounced in agreement, but the sparkle only distracted him a moment before his interest return to his new toy. "Truck." He lifted the four-wheeler off the plastic road—a gift from Santa—and then lowered it again, zooming it along the make-believe highway.

Jon hit a button that triggered a red light ahead.

Joey's eyes widened again. "Stop." He seemed to tell himself as he slowed the truck and paused, giving Jon a smile.

When Jon triggered the green light, Joey eyed him a moment and raced on ahead with Jon's sports car right behind him. As Jon raced around the truck, his brrring sound effect was nearly covered by Joey's giggles.

Neely curled her legs beneath her, a smile stretching her cheeks and warming her heart. Jon had proven himself over and over as a man who loved kids and would be a great father. Her pulse skipped and danced through her heart.

Joey rubbed his eyes with his fist, and Neely glanced at her watch. Ashley had asked her to entertain him while she went to the movies with Erik. So far, the noose hadn't tightened enough to do any damage, but Neely suspected it would happen eventually. Jon's calming effect had stopped her worries, and instead of feeling the angst she'd experienced for so long, she'd learned to hand her worry over to the Lord. Finally she'd found peace. The truth would strike Ashley when the time was right, and Neely's main prayer was that Ashley would not be hurt. Her sister deserved good things after all she'd been through losing Adam.

Her gaze lowered to Joey, and she grinned seeing Jon the only one pushing his car along the plastic highway. "Having fun?"

He looked up and grinned. "Do I look like it?"

She nodded, then tilted her head toward Joey who had gone into his own little trance. "I think it's sleepy time."

Joey's hand slipped off the truck, and he pressed his palms against the floor and rose. When she opened her arms to him, he didn't resist, and she lifted him against her chest. "Want to put on your jammies?"

He nodded, and she gave him a hug. One thing she loved about Joey was, despite his energy, he admitted when he'd had enough and wanted a nap or knew it was bedtime. "I'll be back in a minute."

She carried him into the guest room, slipped him into his pajamas, led him into the bathroom, and then tucked him into the bed along with his favorite stuffed toy. She left the hall light on and the door ajar, then returned to the living room. When she spotted Jon still sitting on the floor, she smiled. "Would you like a set of cars and trucks for your birthday?"

He loaded the last piece of roadway into the box and rose. "I'll think about that. But I'd prefer a sports car I can fit in. Is that in your budget?" He opened his arms, and she stepped into his embrace. Before she could answer the question, his lips touched hers, as if they'd been together forever.

When she caught her breath, she sighed. "Wish I could buy you a car. Even a toy one. Christmas took a bite out of my salary. Did you know a secretary's paycheck looks pitiful?"

His smile faded. "I know. You deserve more, but that's how it is. I suppose looking for another job is on your mind." His body tensed, but he didn't let her go. "Are you thinking about going back to Indian—"

"Not at this point." His face told her what he feared. "I might start looking around here. I have good credentials, and if I don't get my résumé out there, I won't know what's available."

He nodded, his tension lessening as he released her.

She crossed to the sofa and patted the cushion, hoping they had time to talk. She'd grown closer than she ever thought possible, and only occasionally did the memory of a pesky kid enter her mind. But instead of a vivid image, he morphed into the handsome man who gazed at her as he stood beside the Christmas tree.

"Time is flying. We'll be back to work in a few more days." He settled on the sofa and slipped his arm behind her on the cushion. "This has been the best Christmas vacation I've had in years, Neely."

She nodded. "When I worked in Indianapolis, I only had a few days, and I'd make a quick trip here for Christmas Eve and Christmas Day, and then return to my friends and the holiday parties. I know I've settled in, because that seems like a long time ago—nice memories but ones I don't really miss."

"Honestly?" His eyes searched hers.

She tilted her head and brushed his lips with hers. "Promise." She slipped her hand in his. "Did anyone ever tell you you'll make a wonderful father?"

"Me?" He pressed his free hand against his chest. "I don't really have much involvement with kids except the teens at school, and then I'm not sure about fatherhood and dealing with teens."

She chuckled, imagining what it might be like dealing

with the multitude of teen issues she'd gone through growing up. "I think about the age ten you could send them off to boarding school and invite them back a few years later."

Slipping his arm around her shoulders, Jon drew her close his gaze sweeping her face. He brushed strands of hair from her cheek and cupped her chin in his palm. "Sometimes I imagine a daughter that looks just like you."

Her heart spiraled as words failed her. But she didn't need words. His mouth touched hers drawing her away from the world of problems and leaving her floating on a cloud of dreams. When he eased back, his lips still close to hers, she caught her breath. "Jon, I..."

A grin stole to his face. "When you first came home, I had too much to prove to you. I wanted to rid you of those horrible memories of the past and prove I was a man. All that seems foolish now, and I've learned something important."

She could only guess what he'd learned. She studied his face. No tension. No regret. Only a faint grin hanging on the curve of his mouth. "What?"

His smile deepened. "I asked you to call me Jon, and for so long you refused, and what I learned is..." He shook his head and chuckled. "I learned that I miss hearing you call me Jonny."

Surprised, she tilted her head. "Really?"

He nodded. "But I'll take Jon rather than not hear your voice at all."

Every worry she'd felt, every boulder she put in their way as a stumbling block to falling in love, tumbled away. His muscles flexed against her shoulder. His eyes searched hers, and she drank in the sweetness of his presence. "I'll take your request under advisement."

His smile grew and he kissed her again, deeper and

warmer than anything she'd experienced. Ashley had defined love, and for once, Neely faced what true love felt like. The one boulder still remaining in her life was being chipped away. If God could forgive sins and told His children to forgive as He forgave, she prayed that Jon could do just that.

Tonight when she turned out the light for bed, she would pray in earnest that He give her the courage to tell Jon what had stood in their way for so long.

Chapter Sixteen

Jon leaned against the doorjamb, watching his sister and Neely carry in another tray of snacks from the kitchen. Rainie loved to entertain, and since Ty had moved into their new home, the one she would live in once they were married, she had turned into a decorator and hostess. Each change in the decor meant another party to celebrate, but tonight nothing new had been added, except a new year that would make itself known in another hour.

Neely caught his eye and tilted her head toward the latest addition to the buffet table. He eased his way through the group of noisy friends to the spread. "What's the latest?"

She gestured to the fare. "Stuffed mushrooms fresh from the oven, and another batch of saucy meatballs." She knew he loved those, but his stomach let him know he'd already eaten too many. Neely had made the "secret" sauce, but he'd wormed the secret out of her and still couldn't believe what she'd used—a cup of ketchup and a can of diet cola.

With the delicious sauce in mind, he pulled a toothpick from the holder and speared one of the meatballs. Before it dripped, he popped it into his mouth. Unbelievable.

She caught him in the act and grinned. "I knew I'd entice you."

Neely did and in so many ways—her laughter, her kisses, and her simple presence in his life. The more time they spent together, the more he believed she had been a gift from God—the plans God promised from Jeremiah: *Plans to prosper you and not to harm you, plans to give you hope and a future.*

Though he'd accepted their friendship immediately as part of God's plan, Neely had taken her time. Even now she held something back, but he'd put it in the Lord's hands. It was the only way he could deal with it now that his heart and head knew he loved her with the kind of depth the Lord spoke about in the Bible. Many scriptures focused on faith, hope and love, but he knew the greatest of these was love.

As he watched Neely, a frown grew on her face. She slipped her hand into her pocket and pulled out her cell phone. He knew why. Her dad had agreed to care for Joey while Ashley went to a party with Erik while Neely and he had plans to be with Rainie and Ty. Her face darkened, and she glanced his way. Seeing her concern, he drew closer, his heartbeat sending a warning.

"We'll be there in a minute." She clicked off and looked at him, tension filling her face. "It's Ashley. Erik is drunk and he's—" She closed her eyes and shook her head. "I'll explain on the way."

He didn't need more than that. Accident? Stranded? Whatever it was they would leave the party to help Ashley.

With a limited explanation to Rainie, he pulled away from her as she begged them to stay. "It's only twenty minutes before midnight."

"I'll explain later." He drew his arm away. "Please."

Rainie let him go; concern etched her face. He hated walking away without giving her a better understanding of why they had to leave so close to midnight, but too many ears were nearby, and many of the guests knew Erik.

As soon as they pulled away, Jon asked for details.

"Erik drank so much that Ashley suggested they leave the party." She shook her head, her look frantic. "She drove him to her house, because she didn't want to be stuck at his."

He slipped his hand over hers and gave it a squeeze. "That was smart. So we're going to drive him home?"

"I guess, but it's worse." Tears rolled down her cheeks. "Erik took her suggestion as a sexual offer. After they were inside, he got rough with her. I don't suppose he realized it being drunk, but he tore the buttons off her dress and—" She covered her face with her hands. "I wanted him to tighten the noose, but not like this."

Heat tore through him as he gripped the steering wheel. "Whether he realized it or not, Erik's heading into the mire if that's what drinking does to him." His heart raced, picturing Ashley in the horrible encounter. "How did she get away from him?"

"She grabbed her cell phone—I don't know how—and locked herself in the bathroom. I could hear Erik beating on the door."

"Dearest Lord, keep her safe." He stepped on the gas, forcing his foot to keep within a reasonable speed but definitely going over the speed limit. Just before he turned onto Ashley's street he heard a siren. Lights flashed behind him. "Stupid." He pulled to the curb and stopped.

Neely released a moan. "Jon, I'm so sorry that—"

"It's New Year's Eve. I should have known they'd be out in full force." He dug into his pocket for his wallet. "I'm more upset because we need to be there."

The officer appeared at the car window, and Jon handed him his wallet and gave him a quick explanation.

He lowered his head and eyed him through the window. "You're the coach at Ferndale High."

His stomach knotted. That wasn't important. Ashley was. "Yes, sir."

He returned Jon's wallet. "You lead the way."

"Thanks." He handed his wallet to Neely and released a pent-up breath. "Here goes." He rolled away from the curb, the officer following. Erik's car sat in the driveway and they both pulled up in front.

Neely darted from the car, and Jon grasped her arm. "Slow down." They reached the door together. Neely tried the knob. It opened.

Grateful Erik hadn't locked it, Jon stepped inside first and Neely moved aside to let the officer enter before her. Erik's voice sounded from the back, his fist whacking against something. He could hear Ashley's muffled voice but couldn't make out the words.

When Erik saw them, his glazed eyes widened, and he blurted a curse.

"Stand away from the door." The officer's voice overpowered Erik's slurred retort.

Erik looked bewildered, his eyes shifting from Jon to the police. He faced the doorway, swaying, his confusion evident. "You called the police, you b—"

"She didn't, Erik. She should have, but she called Neely."

The officer grasped Erik's arm, but he jerked away, stumbling backward until the wall stopped him. He slipped down the wall to the floor. Jon stood back as the young man unsnapped the handcuffs from his belt, pushed Erik's head downward as he pulled his arms behind him and attached the cuffs.

Tears filled Neely's eyes as she pressed her cheek against the door. "You can come out, Ash. Everything's okay."

When the door opened, Ashley stood motionless, her hand covering her face, her dress hanging askew. Neely opened her arms, and Ashley fell into her embrace. The sisters rocked from side to side, calming each other. "Ash, I wanted to protect you from this, but—"

"It was me. I didn't want to believe you. I'm sorry. I shouldn't have blamed you for what happened. You told me in confidence, and—"

"Don't be sorry, Ash." Neely held her close swaying as a mother would a child. "I knew you'd see the truth. It just took time."

Jon sensed this was a conversation he shouldn't have heard. It fell into his mind like puzzle pieces that needed to be put together, and he feared the picture wasn't one Neely wanted him to see.

He stepped away and spoke to the officer who gave him Erik's car keys. They waited in the living room to see if Ashley would go home with Neely, but she refused, saying she was fine and insisting she needed to be alone. They left reluctantly.

New Year's Eve hadn't ended as planned, but it had begun a new year for Neely and Ashley, one Jon sensed would bring them closer together, and if he ever learned what Ashley meant when she said she shouldn't have blamed Neely for what happened, he prayed it would be a blessed new year for Neely and him, too.

Ashley's words rang in Neely's head. *I shouldn't have blamed you for what happened.* She suspected Jon had heard her, and though she'd found reasons to avoid admitting her involvement with Erik, she knew the time had come.

She'd excused herself from Jon to make hot chocolate after the horrible ordeal, and alone she reviewed all that had happened. The policeman left with Erik, and Jon followed in Erik's sports car while she drove Jon's SUV. As she drove, she'd come to grips with the situation. Tonight she promised herself she would talk to Jon.

When she and Jon arrived home, the house was quiet, her dad and Joey asleep. She turned on the Christmas lights and calmed. The problem with Erik had been resolved before he hurt her sister any more than he already had. She assumed the police would keep him overnight and he'd be free to chase other women—his father's wealth and prestige would influence that—but Ashley would come away intact, hurt maybe, but no permanent damage.

"Are you okay?"

Hearing Jon's voice, she turned from the stove and looked into his concerned eyes. "Sorry. I'm thinking."

He nodded and stepped behind her, slipping his arms around her waist. "I know this has been difficult for you."

She only shrugged, having too much to say. The hot chocolate was hotter than it needed to be. She pulled out the mugs and poured the cocoa into them. She handed one to Jon and carried the other to the living room.

When they had settled, the lights of the tree their only illumination, she blew on the liquid and took a sip, then set it on the lamp table. "Thank you." She studied his gentle face, grateful for his presence. "Once again you were here when I needed you. That's how you are."

His tender smile washed over her. "It's where I'm supposed to be, Neely. Do you understand that?"

"I think I do." The meaning of his words felt like a promise. "You said it was difficult, and that's true, because I feel guilty. You know how I wanted Erik to show his true colors, but I didn't want it to be this way."

"Maybe it had to be this way. Think about it. Ashley might have talked herself out of blaming him again if he'd taken a gentle approach. You know his maneuvering techniques. Tonight what he did can't be excused away, except for drinking, and I know your sister doesn't appreciate that, either."

"She's devastated, and not because of what he did, as much as she'd forgiven him so many times before. Now she knows the truth."

A chill swept up her spine and she took a sip of the hot chocolate, but the icy feeling remained. She knew why. Ashley knew the truth about Erik. Now Jonny needed to know. Her eyes met his, and she patted the cushion beside her. "Sit with me, Jonny." The familiar name comforted her.

He grinned. "I like hearing Jonny again. It's comfortable." He grasped his chocolate and shifted beside her on the sofa. He sipped the drink and set the mug on the small cube her dad used as a coffee table.

He brushed her shoulder, and she leaned forward, letting him encircle her in his arm. Resting her head on his chest, she pulled the story out of hiding. Now was the time. "I need to tell you something, Jonny. Something that will probably disappoint you but something you need to know."

His arm tensed a moment but relaxed as quickly. "Nothing about you will disappoint me, Neely. Nothing."

Having been a good friend—more than a friend—these past months, she doubted him. "I made a confession to Ashley that she turned against me so it's difficult to tell you because you mean so much to me."

His fingers played along her arm, brushing her with a soothing calm. "I'm listening."

"It's about my relationship with Erik." She'd expected him to flinch, react in some way. Her pulse tripped, and she fought a ragged breath wanting to tear from her lungs. Without organizing her thoughts, she plowed into the story. "Erik was the rich boy in town, and he was mine. Country clubs. Fancy home. Promises of a life different than I'd had. I didn't weigh the value. I just plowed in, naive and stupid. Absolutely dimwitted."

"No, Neely. You were mesmerized by a life that might never be without Erik."

"Yes, but one that I really didn't value if I'd thought about it." She studied his face, and saw only tenderness. She continued, getting closer and closer to what he needed to know—her determination to remain pure, Erik's manipulation, her fears of losing him. "I know now it was pride. I didn't love Erik, but I was proud that he'd picked me."

She lowered her gaze, feeling her confession slip to her tongue. "He was going away to college. I couldn't afford to live on a campus. I had to leave home so I registered for class at Oakland University. It's a good college, but it didn't offer me the excitement of living away from home like Erik was doing."

She swallowed. "Erik said he wanted me to guarantee my love for him and to be true to him while he was away. I didn't know how to do that. How do you guarantee love?" Her lungs failed her.

"And Erik told you how." Jonny filled in the blank.

She nodded. "So I gave up all that was important to me, and soiled my—"

Jonny pressed his finger against her lips. "I know about that, Neely. You don't have to tell me."

Her head flew back, her eyes searching his. "You know?"

He nodded. "For years."

Her stomach churned. She felt nauseous. "Erik told you?"

"Yes."

"I suppose he told everyone of his conquest."

Jonny didn't respond. Instead he tilted her head and brushed his lips against hers. "It doesn't matter anymore,

Neely. Erik's conquests didn't ruin anyone's reputation but his own."

"And he cheated on me even though I'd given in to him time after time until I was sick and disgusted with myself."

"That's Erik's modus operandi, my love. He's cheated on most women he's dated. A man like him gives all men a bad name."

"Not you. You're a beautiful man, and—"

"Neely, I'm not perfect. I've done things I'm sorry for, but it doesn't make me who I am. I know the Lord has forgiven my mistakes. When I faced Him with my sins, He forgave me. I had to learn to forgive myself. Sin began in the Garden of Eden. It's part of the human condition. All we can do is strive to learn from our mistakes and not repeat them. You've suffered long enough for yours."

The truth will set you free. Why hadn't she allowed those words to seep into her mind and heart and follow them?

"It's time to let it go. You're pure in my eyes and in God's."

She pressed her lips together, holding back her tears. When she could talk without a sob, she thanked him for reminding her of God's grace. Then she did what she'd wanted to do all evening. "Happy New Year, Jonny." She drew her head upward and pressed her lips against his.

Jonny cupped her head in his hand, his mouth warm and inviting. Every worry and fear swept away in the sweetness of his kiss. Tonight the barriers had fallen, the fears had flown away like startled birds, and her heart sang. Tonight was truly the beginning of a new year—a year of freedom from the past with no more searching for something to fill her emptiness or avoiding love because it meant telling the truth. Tonight she'd been set free.

* * *

"Happy birthday to you." Neely gathered with the others, watching Joey's excitement as they sang the birthday song.

"I'm this many." He lifted three fingers, his grin spreading from dimple to dimple.

Neely studied her sister's expression, a mixture of happiness and sorrow, and she understood. She aimed the camera as Ashley set the birthday cake with lit candles in front of Joey. He puckered not really knowing how to blow out the candles but making a valiant effort. Spittle sputtered from his lips, but Ashley caught it before it landed on the cake. Everyone laughed, even Joey.

Photographs were taken of her dad and his grandson, Ash and Joey, and Ashley took one of her holding Joey with cake on his cheeks. Gifts were opened, cake and coffee enjoyed, and Jonny found his place on the floor beside Joey helping him with a big wooden puzzle, everything a child's birthday should be. All except a father who should have been there to see his son turn three.

She swallowed the thought, her emotions raw from the memories she'd shared with Ashley. Little had been said about Erik, but Neely sensed that when the time was right Ashley would need to give that closure, too. She'd learned that life wasn't always smooth sailing, as the old expression said. Rough winds, storm and tempest tossed the fragile boats they sailed in, but always the promise of a rainbow kept people going. Neely had experienced hers, and she looked at him beside Joey as prickles of emotion skittered along her arms.

Four years. She shook her head. Four years was nothing in the scheme of things. What was important was how years were spent. Even though it had gone unstated, Jonny's love lifted her spirit and calmed her tears. He'd allowed her to confess her past, forgave her without being asked, and held her close as if he also felt her pain.

The pain flittered away day by day since they'd opened their hearts three weeks earlier, a night she would never forget—for the confession as well as Erik's downfall. She'd seen him a couple of times, a new woman on his arm. She always sent up a prayer for the woman, that she would not give in to Erik's wiles without knowing the repercussions.

To this day, she tried to recall what Erik had offered her back then. Remembering, she guessed he'd been less experienced and a bit more innocent than he was today. She assumed with time he'd polished his ability to sway a woman to his needs, but the idea saddened her. Erik, too, was trying to fulfill an emptiness that lust would never fill. Contentment came from within, supported by people who offered love and understanding and a God who offered grace and mercy.

She brushed a tear from her eye, then realized Jonny had been watching her. A couple of neighbors had dropped in with gifts for Joey, and the conversation billowed in the room. Ashley rose from an easy chair. "I'll make more coffee." She beckoned Neely to follow, and in the kitchen, she drew her away from the door. "I haven't talked much about New Year's Eve, I know."

"That's fine, Ash. I don't need to—"

She lifted her palm. "I want to thank you and Jon for coming when I called, but most of all I want you to know I'm okay. I realize Erik was the first man I kissed since Adam. I shared something that had been beautiful to me with a man who didn't understand. I didn't listen to your caution out of my own guilt, I think."

"Guilt. Why?"

"Cheating on Adam." She held up her finger. "I know. Adam's in heaven and wants me to move on in life, and now

I know I can. Erik gave me that, at least. I'm not ready for much more than a friendship right now, but I think you are. I hope you and Johnny are talking about the future, and—"

"I'm confident that he'll say something soon."

Ashley nuzzled closer and elbowed her in the ribs. "I told you so."

She laughed, remembering their talk that seemed so long ago. "I finally told him about Erik and what happened. He already knew."

Her eyes widened. "You're kidding."

"Would I kid about that?"

A chuckle burst from her sister, and Neely gave her a hug. "Living in the past keeps us from growing and experiencing life. I'm ready to live, and so are you. Just slow and easy."

The embrace bound them together, but even more the shared experience bound them for a lifetime. Neely prayed the Lord bless Ashley so that one day she'd find someone worthy of her and Joey. And it would happen, she sensed it.

"Can I help?" Jonny strode into the kitchen, eyed them in their embrace and laughed. "Your dad has made similar entrances and ended what might have been a special moment. I hope I haven't done that."

Neely sputtered a laugh, recalling their kisses ending before they began. "No. Your entrance was perfect. And I don't think Dad will end any more special moments. Not anymore."

He slipped his arm around her while Ashley winged her elbow nearby in a playful jab. "Told you so."

Chapter Seventeen

"Neely, wait up."

She stopped in the school parking lot and turned, her Valentine balloons spinning on the wintry wind.

Jon jogged toward her, a smile brightening his face. He slipped his arm around her shoulders blocking the cold air. He came to her rescue in so many ways not only warming her from the cold but warming her heart from emptiness.

She glanced up, pushing her icy lips into a smile. "What's up with you?"

"Happy Valentine's Day." A gleeful look beamed in his eyes. "I'll pick you up at seven for dinner, if that's good."

"It's fine." She'd already agreed once, and she wondered why he'd forgotten. "Daddy's taken care of tonight. I can't believe he's actually going out to dinner with some cronies. That was a great idea you had taking him to the senior center for lunch."

He shrugged her shoulder. "It's good to reconnect with old friends, and I encouraged him to join their walking club. The exercise is good for him."

Her chest constricted picturing her dad enjoying life again. "Did I tell you this? The other day Dad told me a woman named Alice invited him to some kind of fellowship at her church." She'd reached her car and hit the remote.

Jonny chuckled. "I figured that might happen. Your dad's a good-looking guy." He grasped the door handle and pulled it open. "And an invitation to church. That's a bonus."

She edged onto the seat as the three balloons flapped outside in the breeze.

Jonny grabbed two and shoved them in, but the heart-shaped balloon that said Be My Valentine refused to be captured. He manipulated the string and pushed it inside with the others before leaning over to kiss her. "See you soon."

"Can't wait." Her chest constricted when she looked into his eyes. No matter how many hours, even days, she'd spent in his company the thrill of looking at him never ended. He was special, not only with her, but her dad, sister and Joey. When the Lord gave gifts, He truly gave blessings.

Jonny waved, hunkered beneath his down-filled jacket and hurried off to his SUV as she pulled away. He'd made reservations somewhere but hadn't told her. The only thing she knew was that he'd be wearing a sports coat. She couldn't even guess what he had in mind.

Valentine's Day with all its hearts and flowers had meant little to her over the years. Her friends had spouted their special plans, and she'd seen TV commercials and newspaper ads touting romantic gifts, but the information flew over her head. February 14 meant nothing more to her than it being the day before February 15.

Not today. Today he'd surprised her with the balloon bouquet and the cute heart balloon that said Be My Valentine. She'd been teased by the others in the office, but she'd enjoyed knowing that her life had been changed by Jonny Turner, her best friend's brother.

The reality still hit her on occasion, but instead of grimacing, she always lifted her head toward heaven with a thank you for Jonny being in her life.

Despite the heavy snowfall the day before, roads were clear, and she turned into the driveway, noticing her dad had parked on the street which always gave her a clue that he had plans and didn't want to be blocked in. The change in her dad since Jonny had come into their lives amazed her.

When she stepped inside, a sense of home wrapped around her. She still wanted to get a place of her own, but for now she and her dad had developed a playful relationship that they seemed to enjoy. She told him what to do, and he offered a sarcastic rebuttal. She grinned, recalling some of his comments. If only he'd been able to enjoy her mother's company in the same way.

Pushing the darker memory aside, she tied the balloons to a chair back, slipped off her jacket and hung it on a hook in the laundry room. Giving a final look at the Be My Valentine message, she strode to the living room. "What time are you leaving, Daddy?"

"Can't wait to get rid of your old man, can you?" He flashed her a look that tried to hide his grin.

She arched a brow. "I want to make sure you're gone before my date arrives. I'm too old to have my father tell me what time to get home."

He couldn't hide his chuckle. "I tried to pay that guy to hogtie and keep you. It hasn't worked yet."

She sidled next to him and kissed his cheek. "You can't fool me, Daddy. You'd miss me."

"But I'd gain a son-in-law."

That he would. And she'd have a wonderful husband. Her pulse skipped at the possibility. The comfort and joy, the excitement and fullness radiated inside her. Toting her old attitude, she'd expected marriage to escape her, but the unexpected happened instead when Jonny charged toward her on the football field. That day burned into her memory. It was the day her life had changed.

She strode into the kitchen, grabbed an apple and headed up the stairs. If Jonny planned to dress up a little, she wanted to do the same. She opened her closet and scanned her wardrobe. Nothing jumped out at her. Sinking to the edge of the mattress, she reviewed her dressier clothes. One day she needed to revamp her outfits. She'd lost thirty pounds since she'd come home and started exercising. That was more than two full sizes. Half of her clothes looked as if she'd borrowed them from someone with a larger frame.

After perusing her wardrobe, she pulled out a maroon dress, simple but she liked the cowl neckline and the long sleeves. With a gold necklace and drop earrings, she would look presentable. She lay out the clothes, located her black pumps and a clutch bag, then dropped on the edge of the bed, looking forward to the evening.

When her father's voice reached her, she rose and went to the stairs. "Are you going?"

"Yep. I'm on my way. Have fun." His eyes sparkled, gazing at her from the bottom of the staircase.

"You, too, Daddy."

She stood a moment until she heard the door close. Then she headed for the bathroom and ran water in the tub. A few minutes later, she leaned back against the porcelain, enjoying the scent of lavender.

Her mind had been filled with Rainie's wedding shower which she was hosting in another two months, and a few job openings had come to her attention. Part of her loved being close to Jonny, but the other part faced reality. If she wanted a home of her own, she needed to up her income, but sometimes she pictured living in Jonny's house. All it needed was a little feminine touch. Hers, preferably.

Grinning, she nestled her body deeper into the water, but soon she forced herself to leave the tub behind. Her hair needed a curling iron to control her natural wave, and she slipped into her dress and shoes, attached her jewelry and strode down the stairs, anxious to see the man of her dreams. Jonny had become part of her as easy and familiar as buttering toast.

When his headlights flashed across the wall, she headed for the front closet and pulled out her dressy coat as the doorbell rang. She opened the door, her coat on her arm. "I'm ready." As the words left her, she realized he had his hands full.

She pushed open the storm door, gazing at the lovely bouquet of red and white flowers. "Jonny, they're beautiful, but—" Before she could finish, his lips met hers, the bouquet gripped behind her.

When she backed away, she noticed a heart-shaped box as well, and she grinned. "The flowers are gorgeous."

He handed them to her. "Glad you like them." He strode past her and headed for the kitchen.

She followed, watching him open the cabinet where she kept vases. He pulled one down and set it on the counter. "I'll leave the arranging to you." He turned and spied the balloons. "Be My Valentine."

Seeing the expression on his face, she couldn't control her chuckle. "I am, and on top of everything else—balloons and flowers—you didn't need to bring me candy. Are you trying to fatten me up again?"

He shook his head. "You know how I feel about that." He slipped the heart-shaped box on the table. "Your dad will enjoy some chocolates when he gets home."

"You always think of him." She faced the counter and

placed the flowers in the vase, thinking she'd arrange them later. When she turned back, he'd sneaked up behind her, and now she stood in his arms.

He motioned to the arrangement. "Did you read the note?"

"Note?" She shook her head and pulled the small envelope from the flower bouquet. She opened it and slipped out the card. "Will you be mine?" She grinned. "The balloons asked the same question, and—"

"Not so."

She eyed the heart balloon bobbing from the chair and read the message. "Be my Valentine. Okay, I suppose that is a little different."

"Much different." He brushed her cheek with his finger, his eyes searching hers.

She read the card again. Will you be mine? Her pulse skipped, hoping she wasn't reading something into his question. "You're right."

"Let's have a piece of candy before you answer the question." He handed her the box again, and for the first time, she noticed the cellophane had been removed. "You've already eaten some?"

"Only one piece."

His eyes sparkled, sending her pulse skittering. She lifted the lid, and the air escaped her as she saw what was inside. Where a piece of candy should have been, a small velvet box sat in the middle of the heart. "Jonny." Tears blurred her eyes.

He took the candy box from her hand. "Open it."

As she withdrew the jewelry box, he set the candy on the table, his eyes following each move. She flipped up the lid and gazed at a beautiful solitaire diamond, pink, gold and soft blue refractions glinting from the gem. "Jonny, it's gorgeous."

"You're gorgeous, Neely. The stone is nice." He took the velvet box from her and withdrew the ring. "I've loved you since I was a kid. At first it was a boy's crush and later a dream of love." He curved his hand against her cheek. "But one day, you reappeared in my life, and I knew then it was the Lord's doing. I've loved you since I saw you on the football field."

She melted into his arms and their lips met, exploring the deep emotions bound within them. Neely's emptiness had vanished, and the fullness of life and grace had shown her the truth about lasting love. "I love you more than I can say."

"I've waited a life time to hear those words." He drew her hand into his and slipped on the ring. "Neely, will you be my forever wife?"

"I will with all my heart and soul. I can't wait."

"Neither can I." His lips met hers again, and she glowed in the sweetness. The Lord had given her more than she ever dreamed, a true hero who'd loved her for years and now would love her forever.

* * * * *

RECIPE FROM GAIL'S KITCHEN

Sausage and Bread Stuffing

Neely's father loved her mother's recipe for sausage and bread stuffing. The idea came to me because my husband always makes this old family recipe when stuffing is called for. He bakes it in a turkey or sometimes in a casserole. Either way it is delicious.

Ingredients

1 pound ground pork sausage
1 stick of butter
8 stalks celery, chopped
2 onions, chopped
2 loaves day-old white or wheat bread,
cut into 1-inch cubes and dried
1½ teaspoons sage
1 tablespoon poultry seasoning
1 tablespoon celery seed
salt and pepper to taste
3 eggs, beaten
2–3 cups chicken broth

1. Preheat oven to 350° F. Prepare bird or lightly grease a 9"x13" baking dish.

2. Place pork sausage in a large frying pan. Cook over medium high heat until evenly brown. Drain and set aside.

3. Melt the butter in a large frying pan over medium heat. Place the celery and onions in the pan, and sauté until tender.

4. Mix together the sausage, celery, onions, bread, sage, poultry seasoning and salt and pepper in a large bowl. Add eggs and chicken broth into the mixture. The stuffing should be moist, not mushy.

5. Lightly press the mixture into the baking dish or bird. Bake 1 hour in the preheated oven until the top is brown and crisp.

Dear Reader,

I hope you enjoyed *Her Valentine Hero* as Neely and Jon learned who they were is only a small part of who they are now. As we watched them overcome the worries and secrets, I hope we all learned that secrets can destroy lives and relationships unless we learn to turn them over to the Lord and let them go.

In the novel, you also met Neely's sister, Ashley, and her son, Joey. You will meet her again in the next book in this series, and the same question Neely asked, what secret did her mother hold so tightly, will be answered in the final book in the series. And by the way, Neely's red sauce is a real recipe—a can of diet cola and a cup of ketchup cooked on medium heat until thickened. It's delicious on pork or chicken.

I'd love to hear from you, and by visiting my website at www.gailmartin.com, you can subscribe to my online newsletter and keep up with my books, recipes and a monthly devotional.

Please look for my next release.

Wishing you blessings always.

Gail Gaymer Martin

Questions for Discussion

1. Neely and Jon met again after fifteen years. What changes would you notice when running into an old friend after many years? What besides appearance might be different?

2. Have you ever wondered what happened to people who you knew well from your past? Why do these individuals stay in your memory?

3. Why did Neely cling to the old memory of Jonny, as she called him? Did you spot things about her memory that showed her attitude may have been more playful and less serious? What was the significance of calling him Jon and not Jonny, and why did he decide he liked hearing Jonny?

4. Neely's sister, Ashley, had lost her husband and has been raising their son alone. Have you experienced such a problem in your own life? Do you know anyone who has? How can they make life go on?

5. Ashley said she felt guilty dating again. Why would she feel like this? Is it natural?

6. Why did Ashley turn on Neely when she confessed her sin to her sister instead of supporting her? Can you understand why this might happen?

7. Fred Andrews has a biting sense of humor but do you still find him likable? What has Fred been through that

you can empathize with him, yet admire him? Did he ever make you laugh?

8. Neely's father always said, "Laughter is the best medicine." Why did he have that philosophy? That adage comes from Proverbs 17:22. What does this saying mean?

9. Do you know anyone like Neely's mother, Marion? What characteristics did she have that drove people from her? What would cause a person to behave in that manner?

10. Joey was a precocious child who seemed older than his years. What qualities did you see in Joey that showed his intelligence? Did anything he do make you laugh?

11. What qualities did you admire in Neely? What qualities caused her problems? Can you see any of these qualities in yourself or a loved one?

12. What qualities did you admire in Jon? Did you find any insecurities in him? Why did Jon fear losing Neely as his soul mate?

13. Charities played a role in this novel. In what way? Are you active in charities? If so, how do you contribute? Is your church active in the community? Could your church broaden its involvement in the needs of others? Can you do more to help others?

14. Neely's mother had a secret she was unwilling to share with others? Do you think Neely's father knew the secret? What might be the secret that seemed to affect Neely's mother's life?

COMING NEXT MONTH from Love Inspired®

AVAILABLE FEBRUARY 19, 2013

PERFECTLY MATCHED

Healing Hearts

Lois Richer

Helping people overcome their fears is Nick Green's specialty. Even Shay Parker, whose trust was shattered long ago, can't remain immune to the caring doctor for long.

CATCHING HER HEART

Home to Hartley Creek

Carolyne Aarsen

When Naomi Deacon comes face-to-face with her long-ago summer romance, Jess Schroder, as caretaker for his stepsister, will her tenderness remind Jess of what they once shared?

BUNDLE OF JOY

Annie Jones

Shelby Grace Lockhart and Jackson Stroud discover a baby on the town diner's doorstep. Will the sweet bundle of joy bring them together as a family?

MEETING MR. RIGHT

Email Order Brides

Deb Kastner

The sparks in Vee Bishop's online relationship are as strong as those she tackles as a firefighter—until she discovers who her eboyfriend *really* is!

HOME TO MONTANA

Charlotte Carter

After a rough stint in the army, Nick Carbini knows it's time to go home, where single mom Alisa Machak is on a mission to make this war hero ready to love again.

A PLACE FOR FAMILY

Mia Ross

Newly unemployed, Amanda Gardner is grateful for her childhood best friend, John Sawyer, coming to her rescue. Will he prove to be the strong, solid man she's been searching for?

Love Inspired